L.I.N.

More human than A.I.

Sequel to The Other

by Réal Laplaine

Cover design by Cindy Anderson

Books by Réal Laplaine

Intrusion: A Keeno Crime Novel – Book 1
Quantum Assault: A Keeno Crime Novel – Book II
The One: A Keeno Crime Novel – Book III
The 9th Divinity: A Keeno Crime Novel – Book IV
The Buffalo Kid
Twilight Visitor
Dead but not Gone.
See Me Not
Earth Escape
Woman EX
Finding Agnetha
Deception People
The Other
L.I.N.
When Gods Roar
When Cowboys Fall
V.O.I.C.E.- The Silence is Over!

www.reallaplaine.com

"We are slowed down sound and light waves, a walking bundle of frequencies tuned into the cosmos. We are souls dressed up in sacred biochemical garments and our bodies are the instruments through which our souls play their music."

Albert Einstein

This book is dedicated to my wife, who, as always, remains an anchor in my life and to Greta Thunberg, a 16-year-old Swedish girl who forced the world to look at global warming for what it really is, and who inspired this story.

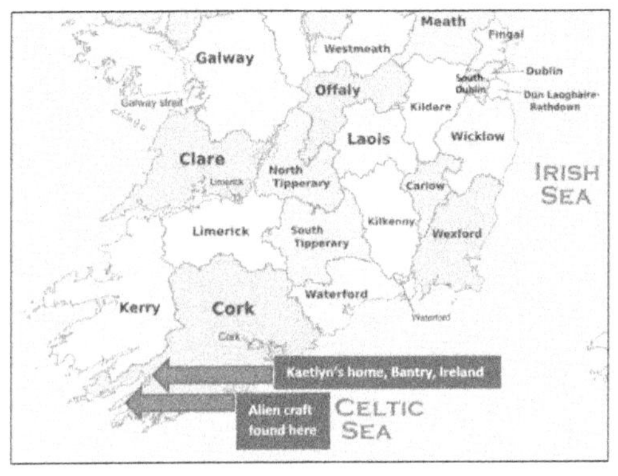
Meath
Fingal
Galway
Westmeath
Dublin
South Dublin
Offaly
Dún Laoghaire-Rathdown
Kildare
Laois
Wicklow
Clare
North Tipperary
IRISH SEA
Carlow
Kilkenny
Limerick
South Tipperary
Wexford
Waterford
Kerry
Cork
Kaetlyn's home, Bantry, Ireland
Alien craft found here
CELTIC SEA

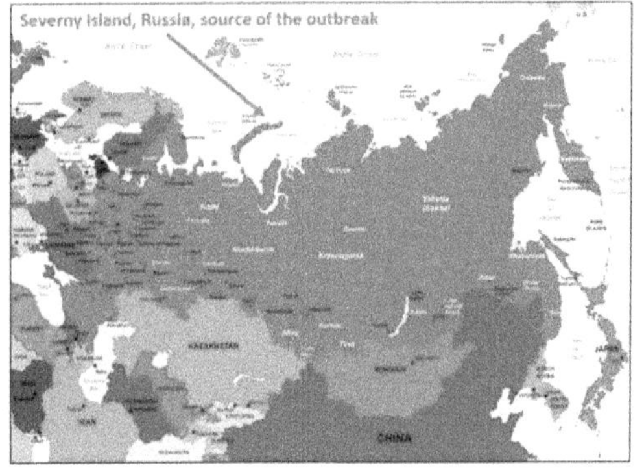
Severny Island, Russia, source of the outbreak
KAZAKHSTAN
CHINA

1 Dublin, Ireland

Serena Bohannon sits down in the last row of the hall at the University of Dublin.

The place is packed, she remarks to herself as her eyes scan the room, with tiered rows of seats set in a semi-circular fashion, facing a stage below.

She came to Dublin to get away from all the drama back in Bantry, where Kaetlyn O'Sullivan, her patient, and friend, and now, a worldwide spectacle, is lying in a hospital bed from a gunshot wound to the head – a bullet that nearly killed her and put her in a coma.

When she received the call just hours ago from Shamus Maguire, Kaetlyn's friend, and partner in crime who had sat by Kaetlyn's side the entire time, refusing to leave her room, relief streamed through her.

"She woke up, Serena," his words still echoed in her head as she sits there waiting for the speaker to begin.

"She insists she needs to get back to the ship right away."

"And the doctors think otherwise, right?"

"They're afraid if she moves it will cause internal bleeding and that could end her."

"She's a stubborn girl."

He chuckles. "Stubborn is a charitable word for it."

"I'm so relieved she pulled through."

"Me too. I have barely slept for weeks," he says with a tired voice.

"Have you heard anything more about … you know?" she asked.

"Not a shite. The military has the place sealed up tighter than a witch's twat…" he paused, "they're not letting any media in, and all I've heard is what you see on the news - two alien crafts hovering over the coast of Ireland – end of story."

"Hasn't anyone approached you to try and get inside the first ship, considering that …"

"You mean because I was there when it crashed?"

"Yeah."

She could hear the frustration in his next words. "They approached me about it, but I declined. I can't remember shite about my past life."

"Not entirely true. You did remember Kaetlyn."

He pauses before answering. "Yeah, but that's different."

"Why, because of the relationship you two had back then?"

"I think so." He pauses. "I mean, doesn't the fact that I was compelled to find her again, after eighteen years, say that love must transcend even the finality of death?"

"Well … it certainly says something."

"That was very 'shrinky' of you, but I appreciate your understanding."

"Don't beat yourself up, Shamus. It takes time. It took days for me to crack through Kaetlyn's amnesia using regressive therapy, before she really started to get a grip on her past life and remember the details, like how to get inside that ship."

"Yuh, I know."

"If you'd let me have a go at you, I might be able to help," she says, knowing already what his response will be.

"Thanks, but no thanks. If I am meant to remember what happened back then, it will come organically, just like I remembered Kaetlyn and what we shared in our past," his final words end with a scent of disappointment.

"Go home, Shamus – get some sleep. I am taking a short respite in Dublin. I'll catch up with you when I get back to Bantry."

After the call was over, and intensely relieved to hear the good news about Kaetlyn, Serena celebrated the day cruising the streets of Dublin, visiting its many charming shops, indulging in some new clothes, a hot lamb stew with a side of taters – the classic Irish dish, and finally, if not ironically, ending up at the steps of the Dublin University where she had spent four years of her life in preparation to become a trauma psychologist.

On a whim she stepped inside and found herself staring at a placard announcing the lecture, happening, as it turned out, just then. She marched directly to the hall and slipped through the doors before they closed.

As the lights dim, an elderly woman, the kind that carries a pedagogic air about them, approaches the podium. “Welcome. The University of Dublin is pleased to have the opportunity to present this speaker to you.” She casts a smile at a woman seated nearby, “In fact, we caught her just before she returned to Canada. So, without further ado, let me introduce, Dr. Dakoda Manning.”

The woman, tall and slim, with sharp angular facial features, long black hair that streams to the small of her back and skin the color of tanned leather, approaches and waits for the clapping to stop.

“I feel a little embarrassed standing here, as frankly, I wasn’t prepared to do a presentation at your notable university. But … now that I am here, you will have to bear with my lack of preparatory detail. Let us talk about Quantum physics for a moment – but from an angle you never considered. Some quantum physicists, such as I, share this idea, maybe it could be better labelled an obsession, that this field offers us windows into other dimensions beyond pure physicality; that QP could be used to open doors to that ever mysterious and so badly understood subject called the human spirit – or to use a simpler term - YOU."

"What do each of us have in common?" She pauses. "Beyond the fact that we all possess a body, and, a mind, although there are different schools of thought on what that is and how it is constituted. Beyond that, we enter a poorly defined field, and yet, it is the most crucial element in the human paradigm - WHO ARE WE REALLY?"

"Ask that question of a scientist and he or she is likely to declare that we are nothing more than the composite of cellular evolution, evolved over a tremendous time, to what we are now. Most of them, if they even acknowledge the factor of a spirit or soul, would relegate that aspect to para-science or religion – not science." She smiles. "Scientists like to deal in facts, and unfortunately, the soul, the spirit and all the other terms for it, is considered not to be science."

"Ask a man of God who we are, and you will generally hear, "a soul" – something that leaves the body and goes some place after death, but beyond that, religion offers no science to back their assertions. You are expected to believe their version, their dogma, their paradigm – no questions asked."

"Now …" she pauses, "ask big pharma that question, you know the pharmaceuticals who are providing all the drugs to keep us "healthy" …" she smiles, "and they, along with many researchers in their camp, and their pockets, will tell you that the net sum of who we are, our qualities, our drives, our passions, our inspiration, et al, is nothing more than synaptic and chemical responses in our brains, all of which can be influenced and controlled with the use of drugs. A platform they use to convince people to buy their drugs." She flicks her wrist. "Naturally, if big pharma ever admitted to the veracity of the human soul as the senior element in the mix, it would put a hole in their titanic profit margin."

She pauses to let that sink in.

"I come from the Indigenous Blackfeet tribe of western Canada. I grew up on an Indian reservation in a remote region of Alberta, where we were taught that our essence transcends purely human existence. Native American lore and mythology, even their beliefs, are also not backed by science. However, that early indoctrination triggered my curiosity, posing the unanswered question – *why has no one proven unequivocally who we are*?"

"We can send rockets and satellites into deep space. We have created technological advances in all fields which stagger the mind, and yet, NO ONE has answered that question, unequivocally, and scientifically."

"As quantum physicists, we set out to prove, unequivocally, using science – not belief systems, not mythology, not religion – but science, WHO WE ARE. We took the most sophisticated and advanced technology in existence today, designed to measure the smallest particulates known, called Quanta, which are, we think at least, the elemental parts that form the atoms and molecules which constitute the Universe around us."

"To put this in perspective, Quantum dynamics is what makes it possible for you to access the entire digital world through the smart phone in your hands. In fact, if you stop to think about it for just a moment, quantum forces are zooming around our heads at a rate and magnitude that defies the imagination, making it possible for billions of digital devices, computers, satellites, and GPSs to function. You do not feel those forces, you do not even perceive them, and yet the incredible power of quantum mechanics is being harnessed in our daily lives to such a degree that the entire infrastructure of our society now depends on something we do not entirely understand and cannot feel or touch. So … if such a force can exist, undetectable to human senses, isn't it entirely conceivable that the forces associated with who we are, are similarly undetectable by conventional means, especially since no one seems to have codified it?"

She presses a remote and points to the screen behind her which shows the image of two rooms separated by a screen. "This simple experiment, which we conducted at the University of Calgary, opened the door to answering that very question. In the room to the right, which is separated by a very thin screen, we set up test subjects and asked them questions designed to get them to think about different subjects. There was no vocalization, they were just asked to think about the questions asked. In the room to the left we set up our equipment, capable of measuring quantum forces insensible to human senses, but detectable at a quantum level. In other words, if something affected or disrupted the Quanta, the machinery would measure it. Through the process of asking people a series of questions designed to evoke different responses and different emotions, we began to see a pattern developing. Quantum physics, as you may know, is based on the theory of energy as both wave and particles."

"After people were questioned, the pattern was clear. Ask a person to think about creation, about love, happiness, and it evokes a measurable response at a quantum level. Ask the same person to think about pain, loss or death, and the response is distinctly different. The spectrum between the two measurements showed that positive things registered most prominently, while negative things, particularly fear, registered the most powerful on the negative spectrum."

She waits for them to digest her words.

"You would be justified in thinking at this point that these measurements were simply a result of output from the brain, and in this, you would be making the same error that other researchers have been making – the assumption that the output from the brain is conclusive evidence that our life-source is situated therein – and it is not."

"Our tests showed, without a doubt, that nearly all of vibrations, frequencies, wave-particle emanations, whatever you want to call them, originated from a source outside the cranium – or at least, not within the brain itself in most cases."

She grins as that statement evokes a sudden murmur from the audience.

"I know, we had the same reaction at first. We checked and rechecked the readings, they were accurate. To make sense of what I am about to tell you, think of this analogy. If the source of our thoughts is separate from the brain, despite what all the authorities are telling us otherwise, then how do we interact with the brain and what then is the function of the brain? The best answer we produced, at least as a platform to work with, was that the human brain is like a switchboard, or like the CPU in your phone or computer, which simply relays the commands given to it when you tap the keypad. You can also think of it like a piano. When you press a key, it strikes a chord which then generates a sound. Think of the brain as the keys, and the chord as the neural-synaptic system which carries messages from the brain to the body. So, then, the big question is, who is hitting the keys?"

She points the remote bringing up image on the screen, showing a body and two circles next to it.

"This is oversimplified, but it serves to illustrate the picture that developed. The large green circle represents WP-1, that is, Wave-Particle-1, while the smaller red circle is WP-2. WP-1 was the wave-particle pattern we measured when we asked people to think about positive things in their lives, such as love, creation, happiness, ambitions, friendship…the future versus the past. All the positive stuff associated with living. WP-2 was the wave-particle pattern we measured when we focused their attention on negativity, such as loss, death, hate, jealousy, and particularly, fear. And as a note, fear was the most potent of the negative factors. As I said, our measurements showed that impulses from these two sources, were coming from a location other than the brain itself. This does not mean that scientific research on the brain is all wrong. As with the analogy of the piano, neurologists have been assuming that the impulses they are measuring coming from certain zones of the brain, is the source, whereas our research shows that those conclusions are short-sighted. The source point is not the brain, once again posing the question, WHO is pressing the keys on the piano?"

She steps closer to the group. "While these discoveries were significant, what is more significant is what they mean. Thought, that is, positive thought, according to our research, is coming from a different place outside the realm of the brain itself. Negative thought also comes from a spot outside the brain, as a separate source. These distances are measured, not in millimeters or inches, but on an infinitesimally tiny quantum scale, but nonetheless, distinct. What became clear to us is that these impulses manifest themselves in the brain as wavelengths, but the brain is not the origin point of our love, our creativity, our impulses, good or bad. So, when scientists say that this or that part of the brain is responsible for your sex drive, your artistic skills and even your most elemental impulses, what they should really be saying is that the brain is simply registering the impulses at that particular point and emanating the commensurate signals to be relayed to the body through its neural highways."

"While our research is not yet complete, we have proposed several postulates. First, that the green circle, is quite likely, the source, meaning, YOU and I, or what others have called the soul or spirit; while the red circle represents something much more visceral, something associated with survival at a baser level, because it seems to be about generating baser impulses such as fight or flight. We have purposely not referred to WP-2 as a mind, or the subconscious mind, to avoid confusing our research with other theories and models. And besides, the definition of a mind, is that element of a person that enables them to be aware of the world and their experiences, to think, and to feel; the faculty of consciousness and thought. Certainly, WP-2, and the impulses it generates, is not a thinking entity, but in comparison to WP-1, seems to be its polar-opposite –

like positive versus negative. For now, until we know more about it, WP-2 remains unnamed.

"Precisely where these two dynamics are located relative to the body, that was, and remains, the subject of more definitive research, because it varied and was not consistent person to person. This suggests that the source, that is, you and I, have our preferences; some of us prefer to be closer to the body, or inside our heads, while others prefer to linger outside. That is hypothesis at this point and subject to further research to corroborate."

"Our research poses some interesting questions. Now that we know with certainty that we are NOT our brains, but something so much more, it changes the paradigms we have been taught to accept. It challenges religious beliefs, scientific models, the medical field and certainly the mental health field, moreover, the very essence of the humanities and how we perceive one another. And now that we know, to a level of scientific certainty, that WP-2 is the cauldron of fear, hate, all the negative facets of humanity, how does this change the optics on good and evil? In fact, doesn't it lend to the philosophical assumption that all people are good, and that the *evil* in us comes from another source entirely? Doesn't this also suggest that by knowing this, we can now address the very source of our fears, depressions, hates, biases, destructive impulses, quite possibly the very matrix of why men fight men in wars and kill one another over stupid things, unlike any other animal on this Earth?"

She pauses as the murmur grows.

"We will be releasing our papers soon. There will be backlash. Authoritative sources will feel threatened by our work will no doubt try to discredit it. Some religious circles will join the fray, perceiving our work as counter to their holy proclamations about a domain that they claim to have sole entitlement over. In the end, truth will and must prevail – and once people see the scientific accreditation, the truth, we're going to see a shift in the zeitgeist of our world."

Thank you for listening."

2 Cork, Ireland

Kaetlyn O'Sullivan presses the last of her things into her backpack and then turns to inspect the hospital room – her home for the past five weeks.

She wonders what awaits her when she steps from the hospital.

A feeling of deep trepidation courses her body as the dull thudding on the side of her head reminds her that just five weeks ago a man fired a bullet into her skull.

The memory is still fresh, even though most of the physical pain has abated, the experience has left a scar on her soul.

It is not death she fears. Recent events, before the shooting, helped her to reconcile that facet of existence, especially after her psychologist, Serena Bohannon, had successfully helped her to navigate the dark realms of her former life, just eighteen years earlier, when she had crashed off the coast of Ireland in the very spacecraft that the Irish military has since exhumed.

What does frighten her still, is that someone from her very village, a man who knew her, had resorted to such violence against her because he believed she was the antichrist.

Just the day before, when news reached the Irish Military, that her release from the hospital was imminent, Colonel Patrick Desmond himself, head of military intelligence at the Irish Defense Forces Naval Base outside Cork, and her closest confident, next to Shamus, Serena, and of course, L.I.N., had shown up to speak to her. She plays back their dialogue in her head.

"I'm glad to see you up and running, lass" said Desmond with a measured smile, although his eyes betrayed a deeper sense of unstated emotion. He had been there, by her side, when the shooter's bullet cracked through her skull. It had been Colonel Desmond, she was later told, who had personally

ordered her evacuated by military chopper to the hospital in Cork and who had put a military detail on her 24/7 ever since.

"Me too."

He offered a smile. "I know you're anxious to get out there, Kaet, but I feel it's in your best interest to know what you'll be facing when you leave this hospital."

"I'm all ears, Colonel."

He glanced at the room and continued.

"The first ship has remained as it was at the time of your …" he paused, "incident. Hovering twenty meters off the ground. It has not budged an inch."

"And the second one?" she asked, having heard about it from Shamus and of course, by watching the news.

"The same. It arrived a week or so after you were shot. It settled in next to the other ship and hasn't budged."

"You've tried communicating with it?"

He tipped his head. "Military and scientific teams have tried all manner of communication attempts, all to no avail.

"What are you thinking, Colonel?"

Desmond shrugged. "Considering that you're the only one capable of communicating to or even entering the first ship, it seems logical to assume that L.I.N. is waiting for you to show up again, you know..." he pauses, seemingly uncomfortable with his words, "...since she considers you to still be the captain of that thing."

"As difficult as it is to accept, my own memories confirm that, Colonel."

He sighed lightly. "I am not trying to negate what you say, lass. Frankly, after what I saw you do last month, well ... you shot a hole in my middle-of-the-road conservatism on the whole subject."

"So, you believe me now?"

He smiles. "I have to no reason to doubt you, and besides, we've been waiting on pins and needles in anticipation of your recovery, so that we can back inside that craft and find out what this second craft is all about."

Kaetlyn sighed as her eyes caught the outline of a military guard hovering by her door. She nodded. "Is that really necessary?"

"Someone did try to kill you, lass."

"And he's behind bars now."

"He is, but as you may know, it's a shite storm out there. Since the second alien craft showed up, extremists, religious zealots, hate groups and nut-jobs around the world have taken license to bandy your name about as a demonic ambassador, as if you are the harbinger of the end of times. So, we're not taking any chances this time."

"Okay," she conceded with another sigh, "so, tomorrow I get out of this place, go home, catch up on

a few things, and then I plan to go straight to the site. What's the plan then?"

"A small team of scientists, myself and Shamus of course, will escort you to the first ship in the hopes that the computer ... L.I.N," he smiles, "plays ball."

"Why wouldn't L.I.N. cooperate?"

Again, he shrugged. "I'm just playing the Devil's advocate, lass. My incredulity was already stretched when we unearthed that spacecraft in the cliffside two months ago. It got tested again when you showed up with a claim of having been inside that thing in your ..."

"Previous life?" she interjected with an impish grin.

"Right, that. Then you break the code, which no one else managed to do, get inside that craft and a whole new level of shite assaults us as ... L.I.N. reveals the nature of your past life mission," he hesitated. "Then of course, there is the shooting."

"Yeah, there is that."

"Anyhow," he continued, "by the time this story is over, the stanchions of my world will have been shaken yet again, of which, I am sure. Right now, the world is held captive by this scene. No one knows what to make of it. Stock markets have risen and crashed more than once in the past weeks as speculations run amuck about the end of the world, alien invasions, you name it. Countless thousands have committed suicide around the globe for fear of the

worst. Countless more have quit their jobs, sold their properties and moved into relative solitude in remote areas or joined survivalist camps. And ..." he drew a deep breath, "there is the bigger issue, the meltdown in the Antarctic and Arctic zones – at an accelerated rate now, and that has the world by the balls as Mother Nature ramps up her own assault. So, to put it mildly, it is a mad-mad scene out there, Kaetlyn, and I just wanted to make sure you were prepared for it."

She nodded. "What about the Americans?"

"Oh," the Yanks, yeah, they're still parked out there off our coast, with an aircraft carrier and two other ships."

"So, they're still laying claim to the alien craft?" She tipped her head, "my ship, actually."

Desmond grinned. "They shot it down some nineteen years ago, so yes, they're holding to their claim according to the conventions of the ´1973 Space Treaty."

"But they haven't made any move?"

He shook his head. "Not since your shooting. Besides, what can they do without causing a shite storm. Both crafts are parked over Irish territory. Storm our beaches and provoke an international incident? The fact is, no one is making any move until we know what we're dealing with." He pinched his lips. "That's why we were so happy to hear that you pulled through this because now we can get inside and speak to L.I.N. again."

Kaetlyn pushes aside the dialogue running in her head, takes one final gaze at the room, and then opens the door.

Claire O'Sullivan sweeps in, embracing her daughter with a smothering hug, while Harry O'Sullivan squeezes her arm. "Glad to see ya stand'n on your own two feet, lass," he says with a broad smile.

Kaetlyn's eyes drift to Shamus, the only person in the entire world who shares the same past-life experience as hers.

"How ya doin'?" he asks.

"My head's still ringing, but …" she shakes a bottle of pain killers at him, "I have feel-good candy to compensate."

As they exit the hospital, a wall of journalists converges, like sharks, all wanting to get the first shots and first words from the nineteen-year-old young woman, Kaetlyn O'Sullivan, the only person to have made First Contact, at least, the only one publicly acknowledged world-wide.

Military personnel move in, forming a wedge and pushing the media back, allowing Kaetlyn and her family to get into the vehicle waiting for them. As they step into the car, Kaetlyn sees a familiar face. Her eyes tear up as her throat chokes.

"I'm so happy to see you," she says as tears pool in her eyes and she leans over to embrace the other.

Serena Bohannon pulls back with a broad smile. “You have no idea how happy I am to see you, Kaet.”

Kaetlyn wipes her eyes and fixes on Serena. “You still want to be my psychologist – after all this?”

Serena flicks a hand to the air. “I just survived five of the most tedious weeks of my entire life, waiting for you to get your sorry arse out of bed. Besides, I would take a bullet anytime over death by acute boredom.”

3 Bantry, Ireland

It is early morning, with a light layer of snow powdering the world, like frosting on a cake.

Kaetlyn eases out of bed, feeling the mild throbbing coming from the hole that is still healing in her head.

A moment later she is staring into the mirror as she gently pulls back the bandage on the side of her head. Until now, she has not wanted to look at the damage caused by the .22 caliber slug that had trenched into her skull, barely missing her brain – one which, no doubt, would leave a prominent scar as a trophy for having survived the incident.

As the protective wrap drops into the bathroom sink, she stares, aghast by the sight of it; ruptured skin, still healing, looked like raw meat being served up on a platter.

Her mind sweeps back to an earlier time when her nocturnal visitor, the specter from her past, had encroached on her world to the point of becoming a crisis in her life. At the time, she did not know what it was or why it came to her so often. It seemed like a nightmare, but at the same time, it also was a calling – as if a voice beyond a veil was desperately trying to reach her.

It wasn't until she sat down with Serena Bohannon, her therapist, and not because she chose to, but because her school had temporarily suspended her until she was deemed fit in their eyes, that the weave and tapestry of this strange vision began to unravel – and within weeks, they had not only discovered that she was getting flashbacks from an earlier life, just eighteen years before, but that the surrealism of it all was now compounded by the fact that the Irish military had simultaneously discovered an alien craft embedded in a cliffside off the coast, not more than forty kilometers from her home – her craft, as it turns out, the very one she had died in when it crashed.

A knock to her bedroom door pulls her back from her mental maundering.

"Kaetlyn – breakfast is ready," announces her mom.

"Be right there, mom" she answers as she applies a new bandage to her wound.

Arriving to the kitchen she notices the dour look on her dad's face, and the equally concerned one gracing her mom's. They are like reading the pages of a book, their emotions, and thoughts as lucid as the words written therein.

She smiles. "Calm down, you two – I'll be okay."

Harry O'Sullivan drops his paper to the table with dramatic effect. "Calm down! You nearly died. If you think you are goin' out of this house without me, forget it!" he announces. "I'm goin' with you today, and anyone so much as looks at you the wrong way, I'll drop 'em with this," he announces with a raised fist.

Harry has been living his own nightmare these past weeks, as Kaetlyn lay in a coma, fighting for her life. Just before her shooting, he had faced off with the very man who had put a bullet in her, a hypocritical loudmouth and religious fanatic, named Stan Murphy, who lived in Bantry and who called Kaetlyn a witch to Harry's face. Harry knocked him to the ground with a powerful southpaw to the jaw, but ever since, he regretted not having done more.

While Murphy had been convicted for attempted murder, it was Harry who had to live with the feeling that had he done more, Murphy would never have had the opportunity to hurt his little girl.

Claire raises a hand. “Please, Harry, we’ve had enough violence.” She turns to her daughter. “You are sure you are ready to go there? You still look a little peaked, honey.”

“I’m fine, really,” answers Kaetlyn as she butters up a hot scone and takes a bite. “Hmm, you’ve outdone yourself, mom.”

Her mother offers a weak smile. “I used more butter than usual.”

The doorbell rings and a moment later her mom returns with Shamus Maguire.

“Take a seat,” commands Claire as she prepares a cup of tea for him and then shovels two scones onto a plate and lays it in front of him.

Shamus offers a tepid smile at Kaetlyn. There is so much he wants to say to her, so much he has been holding back these past weeks as he sat by her bedside, waiting, hoping, and praying that she would wake up from her coma.

Kaetlyn senses his anxiety. “Hi ya, Shamus. Eat up – we’re leaving soon.”

“We?”

Kaetlyn tips her head at her father whose face remains grim as he pretends to read his paper.

“Ah, the security detail.”

“Aye.”

Harry lowers his paper again. “Have ya even considered that maybe you won’t get back inside that thing.”

"Nope," answers Kaetlyn.

"But, what if that other craft, the bigger one, is somehow telling that smaller one not to cooperate with you."

"Why would it do that, dad?"

"D'know, just seems kind of fook'n weird that the second ship comes here and does noth'n, noth'n at all."

Kaetlyn shrugs. "What do you expect."

"Maybe … ask to see our leader," he offers with a smirk.

"You've been watching too much telly, dad."

"Colonel Desmond told me, in confidence," begins Shamus, "that the predominant theory is that they are simply waiting."

"For what?" asks Claire.

Shamus tips his head at Kaetlyn. "For her to come back."

4 Kilcrohane, southwest coast of Ireland

As Kaetlyn steps from the vehicle, her eyes are uncontrollably riveted by the sight, which until now, she has only seen on television.

The smaller craft, which she is already familiar with, since she had been its captain in her former life, is dwarfed by the one next to it, easily three times its size.

While the smaller one is shaped like a dolphin, that is, smooth and elongated, the second and larger craft looks more like a donut, minus the hole. It hovers equidistant from the first, high above the shore.

As she watches, there is not the slightest waver or quiver from either, despite the force of a powerful Celtic wind pounding into the shore, in fact, so strong that she is forced to lean into it.

There is not an audible sound to be heard from either craft as they hang there, as if suspended by an invisible thread from the heavens above.

There is something mesmerizing about it, even for her.

Colonel Desmond, head of Irish Military Intelligence, breaks away from a group and approaches her, a broad smile on his lips as his eyes follow her stare.

"Wonderful to see you, lass."

She sighs and lowers her eyes to meet his. "When do we go up?"

Desmond offers a mollifying smile. "Straight to business, uh?" He leads her to a small group standing nearby and begins the introductions. "Prime Minister, this is Kaetlyn O'Sullivan."

Kaetlyn is momentarily struck, as the Irish Prime Minister, Dorothy Malone, extends a hand with a friendly smile. "Nice to finally meet you, Kaetlyn.

When I heard you were going to be here, I had to come and meet you and see for myself what will happen next."

"Thank you, ma'am. I hope you will not be disappointed," answers Kaetlyn.

"I must tell you," Says the PM, "I am impressed by your courage, after what you endured."

Kaetlyn shrugs. "Maybe others are smarter than me."

Dorothy squeezes her hand in a motherly fashion. "I doubt that my dear, I very much doubt that."

Desmond tips his head at the next man. "This is Admiral, Malcolm Calhoon, the Irish Joint Chief of Staff."

The military man, stiff and straight-backed, like the trunk of a tree, offers a temporal smile. "Happy to see you back on your feet, lass. We are looking forward to what comes next."

Desmond continues, introducing the head of the science team, and finally tipping his head at the remaining person. "No introduction necessary here."

Kaetlyn steps up to Serena and squeezes her hand. "I'm so happy you're here."

"Wouldn't miss it for anything," responds Serena.

Moments later, the team is standing on a small platform as the industrial lift rises into the air, one that has been modified. Instead of a screen mesh for sides, it is now reinforced with metal plates, just in case a madman decides to take another shot at Kaetlyn.

As they ascend toward the smaller of the two crafts, old man Celtic Sea buffets the rig with a blast of angry wind, giving everyone a fright.

The operator deftly edges the platform to within inches of the portal.

No one says a word as Kaetlyn, hesitant at first, steps to the edge of the gate and reaches out with one hand, gently sweeping her palm over its smooth obsidian-like surface with a lover's touch. She draws a deep breath, as if the moment is closure from her near-death episode weeks before.

She turns an eye to Colonel Desmond and smiles. "No one's shot me yet, Colonel," she says with an impish flick of her brow, then turns to the ship, places her palm against the portal, taps in the coded sequence – and steps back as the door sweeps silently to one side.

5

For Desmond, Shamus and Serena, the astonishment of being inside an alien craft has lost its shock value, but to the team of three scientists who linger behind, the impact, the utter surrealism, that they are standing inside an alien spaceship, is clearly overwhelming.

As Kaetlyn approaches the control console, Serena comes nearer.

"How you doin,' Kaet?"

"A bit nervous."

"That's understandable."

Kaetlyn grins. "Your bedside manner is pathetic," she flicks her a playful smile.

She pulls herself up onto the large seat, feeling awkward, like a small child trying to negotiate an adult-sized chair.

Drawing a deep breath, she places her hand to the console. The hologram suddenly flashes above them, with the image of L.I.N., the ship's A.I. computer, with her braided silver hair flowing gracefully behind her head, a face, human-like, and yet not, with a more pronounced forehead, protrusive cheekbones, deep emerald eyes, and a slim upper torso, all of it, unequivocally feminine.

"Hello, Kaetlyn, nice to see you back. You seem to have recovered from this unfortunate incident."

"Hi, L.I.N. Unfortunate, yeah."

"I have been tracking your progress. I expected to see you soon enough."

"Good to know. So …" Kaetlyn pauses, feeling somehow uncomfortable about her next question, "what about the other ship out there. Why is it here?"

"Oh, that," casually comments L.I.N., as if it is a minor detail. "I requested it."

Kaetlyn's head rocks with a confused look on her face. "Requested?"

"If we plan to go through with the original mission, we'll need the delivery system to deal with global warming." She pauses to study Kaetlyn. "You really don't remember the details of our mission, do you?"

Kaetlyn's head wags. "No. I'm still trying to cope with what I have remembered so far. So, what does that other ship do? I mean, are there others on board or what?"

L.I.N. shakes her head. "It is merely a drone containing delivery pods, that is all."

"Delivery pods?"

"While you were convalescing in the hospital, I completed an analysis on the current state of state of global warming and then requested the precise delivery system necessary to deal with it…"

"But pods – what pods?"

"The pods contain the nanorobotic entities, or BioBots, that will clean up the CO2 emissions causing global warming."

"Okay. And you said you requested this drone … from who?"

L.I.N. raises a questioning brow. "Your employer, of course, the very people who sent you here," a statement which momentarily gums up Kaetlyn's head.

L.I.N. takes the window of opportunity to turn to the others. "Hello, Colonel Desmond," she nods.

"Hi, L.I.N."

"Mr. Maguire, nice to see you too."

"You too," he responds.

"I know you attempted to enter the ship while Kaetlyn was convalescing. Unfortunately, without the proper coding, the ship's security protocols will not comply, and …" she pauses to study him a second, "unfortunately, your current physical state does not match the one you possessed before."

Shamus waves it off.

"And Serena – lovely as always," says L.I.N.

Serena smiles. "Happy to see you too, L.I.N."

"And these people are …"

"Scientists," answers Colonel Desmond. "They are here to observe and ask questions, if that is acceptable to you?"

L.I.N. offers a dismissive shrug, a gesticulation she picked from Kaetlyn who does it often. "If the captain agrees, I am fine," she turns an eye to Kaetlyn who simply shrugs, as usual.

"I assume you've been tracking the disastrous meltdown of our polar ice caps, and the dramatic effects it is already having on our world."

“I am up to date on all facets of global warming, Colonel, and there is still a small, but diminishing window of time to deal with it.”

“How small?”

L.I.N. tips her head to one side as another holographic projection appears. “This graphic illustration provides a fairly accurate analysis of how much time you have before global warming exceeds the threshold where there is simply no turning back.”

“Why is that?” asks one of the scientists.

“Once a planet such as yours, overheats, it begins its own process to restore balance and there is no technology that we know of that can stop a process of such magnitude. Had we addressed the matter eighteen years ago, as originally intended with our mission here, the window of opportunity would be far greater. Unfortunately, you chose to shoot our ship from the sky.”

“For the record, we didn’t shoot your ship down, that was the Yanks...”

L.I.N. cuts him off. “I know the details, Colonel, nonetheless, the governing powers have failed to listen to the science – ample evidence that should have compelled much more action.” She points to the holo as more visuals appear. “What you see and hear about are icecaps melting, changes in weather, brutal storms, heat waves, but what you do not hear about and what is most important, is that your oceans are warming at an alarming rate, and this is killing off countless life forms, the elemental necessity that results in oxygenating your world, of which 70% of the oxygen comes from those very oceans. At their current rate of warming, countless species, both creatures and plant, will perish in the next couple of years, and that means much of your food source will also disappear."

A quiet sigh could be heard permeating the group.

"At this point of declination, the delivery system in that drone," continues L.I.N., "will only work if you dramatically reduce carbon emissions on a planet-wide basis. Failing that, anything we would attempt would fail, because continued green housing would counter the efficacy of the BioBots."

"How does the delivery system work?" asks another.

L.I.N. flicks an eye to the changing projection next to her. "You're familiar with nanotechnology, no doubt?" she raises a brow.

The scientists all nod in unison.

"The drone contains pods, thousands of them, each of them filled with millions of micro-nano-bio-bots, which, when deployed in the upper end of your stratosphere, engage a process like what you call, photosynthesis. Like the trees and plants in your world, the bio-bots are designed to absorb CO2 and sunlight to produce clean energy – eventually, over years, they remove the excess gases choking this planet."

"But how do they stay up there, how do you control that?"

"Every cluster of BioBots has a central nanorobotic control unit that keeps each cluster geo-synched and together, precisely where they are meant to be – so they don't disperse."

"And how long do they stay there?"

"While a small percentage of the BioBots do disintegrate and fall away, in the main, the cluster remains intact for a period lasting up to seven years."

"And what happens to the bots that fall to the Earth?"

"They are bio-degradable and harmless to the eco-system, and, moreover, even if inhaled by living creatures, are expelled by the body as a natural part of its cleansing process."

A scientist approaches the holographic image, showing a simulation of the bio-bots. She points. "And you've tried this process? It actually works?"

L.I.N. raises a brow. "You're not the first civilization to have nearly destroyed its world in this manner."

She is met with blank stares.

"There are countless civilizations out there, some of them …" she pauses, "just as irresponsible as yours, having abused their world to the point of systemic collapse."

"So, if this had been started earlier…" begins Desmond.

"Then, the margin for permeation of the bio-bots would have been wider and longer and the degree and duration of the cooling effect would have been more tempered. As it is," she nods at the changing holographic projection next to her, "and for this to be successful, you will need to dramatically reduce carbon emissions."

"How dramatic?" asks Kaetlyn.

"By my projections, no less than 85% of your current output, and that is a charitable estimate.

Kaetlyn sighs and utters, nearly hushed. "Now, I don't feel so bad about screwing up my mission," she flicks a brow at Shamus."

L.I.N. responds. "The planning for our mission was faulty, Kaetlyn. It failed to assess the degree to which the current Earth society was and would continue to pollute its atmosphere. So, no, Kaetlyn, your premature death did not commit this world to its current fate, although, it would have been better had we started this process, somehow, two decades before now."

"You're suggesting that we'd have to get all the major players together and get them to agree not only to this intervention of which you speak of," says Desmond, "but to also accomplishing a major reduction in carbon emissions?"

"Correct."

"But, even if we could get everyone on board with such a program, it would take years to switch over to other forms of energy that do not add to the greenhouse effect."

"You said the bots are designed to stay up there for seven years, how long, exactly, are we talking, in terms of having to wait out this permeation process with these … bio-bots?" asks a scientist.

L.I.N. raises a brow. "Once we deploy the bio-bots, the process will take a minimum of 5.8 years before your world has reset itself – that is, where planetary temperatures return to normal. That figure assumes that current emissions of greenhouse gases is reduced by no less than 85% its current levels."

"And how long, by your estimate, do we have before global warming hits a point of no return?" asks Kaetlyn.

"Six to eight months – give or take a few."

"So, we really have no time left. We have to act now."

"That is correct."

6 The White House, Washington

Since the attempt on Kaetlyn O'Sullivan's life, over a month earlier, President Tamp had ordered the US military to back down on its efforts to recover the alien craft.

The optics were simply not good, given that the girl at the center of the storm had been lying in a hospital bed – her future uncertain at best.

President Tamp turns to the Madox P. Riley, Chairman of the Joint Chiefs of Staff.

"I saw the news. The girl has recovered, and she took a team of people inside the craft. None of our people were there," his tone betrayed his disgruntled mind.

"Yes, timing is critical now."

"Now?!"

Madox tempers his approach, seeing that the man is edgy at best. "Sir, we know that ship, that computer, possess technology that will be a game changer. Everything from being able to transform solid matter into something else, which it used to hide itself for two decades in the side of a cliff, to a hull that resists all attempts to penetrate it. Those two pieces of the puzzle would change the technological curve for any nation that gets hold of it."

"You don't have to convince me that it belongs to us, what you need to convince me of is how the hell to do it this time without being compromised or letting the whole goddamn world watch, like that whole theater up in the North Sea."

Madox nods. "That was classifiably FUBAR, but we learned something valuable from that whole encounter with the Russians."

"What?"

"The alien craft can be disabled with a strong electromagnetic force, as we know from having shot it down nineteen years ago, and as recent events proved, a strong enough EMP can also activate its defense protocols, as proven by the underwater explosives set off by the Irish and British, which forced the alien craft to evacuate the area."

"Get to the point, Madox."

"Given a controlled EMP, just enough to jump-start the alien craft, but not disable it, we could force it to take the same evasive action it did when it took off from the Russian trawler. We know that its onboard computer has a directive of some kind, to protect the ship, that's already evident, so if we cause a blast in the vicinity of the craft, it should force the computer to do the same thing again."

"But how do we control where it goes?"

"We don't have control of that factor," answers Madox, "and I would like to ask Admiral Willis of the Air Force, to explain this further."

Admiral Willis begins, "Mr. President, are you familiar with ADX?"

"They're some kind of military contractor, that's all I know."

"Correct, sir. ADX was formed under the umbrella of the Air Force in 1995. We gave them the kickstart they needed, and now, they operate as a private contractor, with one exclusive client – the US military."

"Okay."

"We started ADX because we needed a place to storehouse and develop technology that was off the grid."

"What technology?"

"Since the mid 1940's, the Air Force has been collecting alien artifacts. Bits and pieces, and even…"

The President manifests sincere surprise. "You mean you actually have alien stuff. Area 51 is not just a hoax?"

"Area 51 exists, but that is not where the real stuff is kept anymore. ADX was created by us, to move the whole subject away from our bases, and with one mandate only; to repurpose alien technology and weaponize it to put America's military ahead of the curve."

The President's head sits askew as he listens.

"Over the years, ADX has developed and refined advanced weaponry, one of them being a very powerful EMP cannon, which they call Big George, and a guided missile, the ADX-SR, which travels at speeds that no other nation can match, and moreover, is undetectable by conventional means."

"Big George?" chimes the President with a raised brow.

Willis smiles. "A term of endearment, that's about all I can say. Anyhow, the plan is to use the ADX-SR missile to set off a powerful EMP in the vicinity of the two crafts, forcing them to take evasive measures and evacuate the Irish coastal area. The blast also releases tiny nano-particulates which will append to the alien crafts, allowing us alone to track them."

"Like a GPS?" asks the President.

"Same concept except these particulates are sensitive to tracking equipment devised by ADX."

"So, basically, you want to spook this computer, this L.I.N., into evacuating the area and then what?"

"Once we know where they land, we hit them with a secondary EMP, but this time strong enough to disable the computer. Then we collect them up, get them to the nearest military base, and let ADX dig into them."

The President turns to the Chairman of the JSC. "General?"

"It's a plausible plan, sir. The critical part will be getting to them fast enough to execute the next phase."

"But how can you be sure the ship's computer won't resist."

"Mr. President," begins Admiral Willis, "There are a lot of factors we don't know at this stage, but we do have the most advanced EMP device in the world, and we know how to use that effectively. We're going to do our best educated guess."

Tamp's face sobers as he thinks about the prospects of making it to a second term in office as President. If the alien crafts end up in Russian or

Chinese hands, or worse, North Korea, he will not see the back door fast enough as it hits him in the ass.

He looks at the Joint Chiefs. "Do it – but don't fuck it up."

7

Colonel Desmond pokes his head into the hut where the three are sitting romancing hot cups of coffee. "Are you ready to go back up?"

Kaetlyn shrugs. "Course we are!"

"Good," he says as he steps in, "because the PM wants to speak to L.I.N. herself."

Once again, escorted by armed guards, and a biting winter wind to bat, they arrive at the lift where they meet the Prime Minister.

"I have to tell you," Begins Dot Malone in a whispering tone to Kaetlyn, "I'm practically shite'n m'pants at the thought of doing this."

"Nothing to be nervous about, ma'am."

Dot straightens. "Easy for you to say," she steals a glance upward at the two ships hovering in the air. "My first go at ET."

Dot Malone wraps an arm around hers and together they turn and step onto the lift.

Kaetlyn feels the eyes of the entire world are on them, and indeed, on the cliffside overlooking the beach, and countless satellites orbiting high above, millions upon millions of people are watching.

As they rise into the air, old man Celtic delivers a brutal gust that shakes the lift like a flower in the wind, just to prove once again that this is his domain.

The PM grips Kaetlyn's hand. "Where is your friend, the other one?" she asks, her eyes nervously flitting back and forth as the world seems to shake.

"You mean, Shamus?"

"Aye."

"He wanted to sit this one out."

Dot's eyes drift toward her. "Has he remembered things, like you?"

"Bits and pieces. He is still trying to make a connection to his past life. Hopefully, as we progress, he'll start to remember more."

"And what exactly was his role on the ship – you know, back then?"

"He was the ship's engineer."

"And you were …"

"The captain and lead scientist," answers Kaetlyn with a tepid smile.

"And there were three of you on this mission?" she raises an incredulous brow.

"Yes."

"Three people to save a world. Seems a little underrated."

Kaetlyn chuckles. "It should have been enough, had I done my job."

The lift jerks suddenly to a stop, and sways to the force of a billowing wind.

Kaetlyn promptly places her hand to the hull, taps in the code and steps inside with the same casual demeanor as if she were entering a food market.

Moments later they are facing L.I.N.

“Hello, Kaetlyn.”

“Hi, L.I.N. This is Dorothy Malone, the Irish Prime Minister. She would like a word with you.”

L.I.N. nods at the woman. “Nice to meet you?”

Dot momentarily struggles with the fact that a living computer is addressing her. “Likewise,” she answers, and please, just call me Dot.”

L.I.N. nods. “What would you like to speak about?”

“After listening to the briefing by the others who met with you earlier this day, I came to the rather frightening conclusion that someone will have to bridge your message to the leaders of other nations.”

“I would agree with that conclusion.”

The PM nods at Kaetlyn, with a diplomatic smile. “Not that I think Ms. O’Sullivan is not up to the task, but given recent circumstances, I think it might be best if someone else, someone already inside the political arena, acts as ambassador.”

“Again, I would agree,” answers L.I.N. “So, assuming we are preparing you for such an ambassadorial mission, what can I help you with?”

"Well …" the PM pauses to gather her thoughts, "this is a tough crowd. Not only the politicians but the people they represent. I need to be well prepared, and to do that, I must understand how precarious our situation is."

"You require more facts?"

"I do."

"In addition to what I have already related to the others, I have done an independent analysis of carbon emissions in your atmosphere, which confirms what your scientists have been saying of recent, showing it to be at over 450 parts per million."

"I am familiar with that datum," responds Dot.

"Yes, no doubt you are. However, what your scientists do not know, and which I have recorded in my extensive data banks, is that when the CO2 levels surpasses 550 parts per million for a planet such as this, there is no turning back. Such a concentration of carbon emissions, permeating the atmosphere, has a catalytic effect – the planet will react, and it will be a dramatic kick back – one you are not likely to survive."

"How dramatic?"

"Like nothing you have experienced before. Raging fires all around the globe, torrid conditions and brutal sweeping sandstorms which choke entire continental zones, shifts in weather that will undoubtedly affect global agriculture resulting in massive food shortages and starvation on a scale unseen before. Shall I go on?"

Dot draws a breath. "No, the picture is rather vivid." Her head bobs as she weaves through a storm of questions. "We all know that the largest polluters are the most resistive to change."

"Indeed," answers L.I.N., "considering that two nations alone are responsible for nearly 40% of the CO2 emissions resulting in global warming."

"America and China, correct?"

"Yes," L.I.N. answers with a tip of her head. "And when you consider that the United States, which constitutes less than 4% of the world's population is contributing 14% of the toxic emissions into the atmosphere, it is quite disproportionate to the rest of the world."

Dot draws a breath. "They have already proven to be uncooperative in the matter of global warming sanctions, so the very idea of trying to get them to reduce CO2 emissions by 85% or more, makes me feel that climbing Mount Everest would be simple in comparison."

8

The first day back in action left Kaetlyn feeling both exhausted and lost, as if she is floating aimlessly in another dimensional reality; a place where her current life merges with her past one – like water mixing with mud.

Nothing is quite clear.

Sitting there, listening to L.I.N. engaged in dialogue with the Prime Minister, had stirred the soup of her past with the reality of the now – and she was not sure if the emotions she felt were real or just impressions from the past.

One thing was for sure, her stomach felt like a brick, as anxiety peaked about the prospects of the future role, she might play in saving a world from the brink of disaster.

Her parents are silent as they navigate their way through the mass of cars and people – a literal throng that crowds the narrow streets of Bantry, a place that can hardly be called popular, except in the summer during beer fests and other local events that attract tourists.

Once home, she plunks into bed and lays there, trying to clear her mind just enough to permit sleep to take her.

Reflecting on the time, nineteen years ago when their ship, her ship, was shot down by an

American satellite, and then crashed off the coast of Ireland, where she and her crew mates had expired, it all seemed so surreal – and yet, every minute of every hour, says otherwise.

What were they thinking? she wonders. *Sending us to a hostile planet like this one, and expecting us to passively inject the bio-bots into the atmosphere and hope to shift the course of a world, without really being noticed?*

Despite attempts to mollify her sense of responsibility, she cannot evade the reverberating voice from her conscience, the one reminding her that as the captain of that mission, her mandate was, first and foremost, to assess the current state of Earth and its culture, and then to advise her Command, based on that analysis, of the best approach to dealing with the planet's situation. She failed to that, she had overstepped her bounds by permitting the ship to get too close to the planet without assessing the exact state of its defense systems – a deadly error that cost them their lives and the mission – and now, the very survival of this planet – now her home.

She sighed as a wave of guilt steeped in her soul, like a smoldering brew of toxicity.

Her phone buzzes. "D-TEKT, whose messaging me?"

"Shamus Maguire."

"Play it."

"Kaet. Know you're probably trying to rest; was hoping we could sneak out and take a pint somewhere, just you and I. Call me if you are up for it."

She lay there in the dark for a time, staring at the ceiling – debating whether she should sleep or meet up with Shamus. The decision came as quickly as the thought, sleep seemed as evasive as dust fairies, leaving only one option.

"Going out with Shamus," she announces to her mom and dad as she dons her winter gear.

"Need a ride?" asks Harry without looking up from his paper.

"I'm fine, dad."

"Watch out for the damn sharks."

Kaetlyn knows he is referring to the reporters who lurk the streets, like paparazzi, hunting for a new picture of *Star Girl*, the girl who talks to aliens.

She exits through the back door, hops a small fence, and walks away without being noticed by the media vans parked out front.

It takes only minutes to arrive to the center of town. Clustered within its narrow streets are pubs, a coffee shop, a bakery, a grocery store, the post office, and of course, Bantry church, all the elements of a typical Irish town.

Ma Murphy's Pub stands alone on one corner, shining like a beacon in the dark.

Kaetlyn steps inside, shakes off a new layer of snow and looks around for the familiar face. Eyes suddenly fix on her as the sound of voices edge down to taciturnity, a discomforting silence as they stare at her as if she is nothing more than a circus act, a spectacle or even, the object of their disdain.

They remind her that the man who tried to kill her just five weeks ago, was a patron of this very pub, a long-term resident of Bantry, and of course, a racist and extremist who no one would dare call a terrorist, being a god-loving Catholic and all, but nonetheless, he pulled the trigger – *so what's the difference who he worshipped*, she thought.

A hand grips her arm causing her to jump slightly. She turns to see his smiling face.

Shamus glares back at the eyes looking their way and a second later, the noise and clatter of a dozen voices fills the air once again.

He leads her to a table in the far corner and then returns a moment later with two pints of ale.

"Don't worry 'bout 'em," he nods toward the cluster sitting further away. "You're a celebrity now, comes with the territory, Kaet."

"Celebrity. Fook that!"

"Just accept it and you won't have a problem with it."

She shrugs.

"How'd you get on with the PM?"

"It's progress, I guess. The PM is honestly looking at how to present our case to the world."

"Wow, hard to believe that in just a few months it's come to this."

"How are you doing with it all?"

Shamus rolls his eyes. "To be fair, I'm still struggling with the whole fook'n thing, like I wake up sometimes and think I must be in a dream – that none of this can be real."

"Join the club." She takes a sip on the ale.

"So, do you think we can do it, can we stop the global warming at this point, or not?"

"It's tighter than a gnat's ass." She sighs. "If only we had accomplished our mission back then, things wouldn't be so bad now."

"You do not know that, Kaet. Frankly, without more reconnaissance on this culture, how the fook were we supposed to succeed anyhow?"

Kaetlyn's forehead bunches up. "That is my point, I should have known. It was written in the mission mandate. Observe, analyze and report – those were my mission orders. If I had followed protocol and kept us further back and just done that, we would have found out pretty fast that they had military-grade satellites in orbit and that would have changed everything."

"You are missing the real point here. Whether or not we discovered the military satellite before it shot at us, the real issue is exactly what we are facing now –

the resistance to change, the superpowers who refuse to take global warming seriously. If we had done more observation back then, we would have known what we were up against. That would have taken an on the ground analysis of the situation, which was probably beyond the scope of our mandates at the time."

Kaetlyn smiles at him. "You're always trying to encourage me, keeping me looking at the positive side."

"I always was the optimist, and you, the realist."

"You remember that about us?"

"I do. Even back then, when we were …" he pauses for the right words, "a couple, you were the realist, and I was the dreamer."

"You seem to remember so much more about our relationship than I have, and yet, you're still struggling with remembering other details."

Disappointment washes over his face like the sweep of an artist's brush. "I wish I could be more help to you and the others, but I just don't remember the details of my past like you do."

"Is anything coming back?"

"When I'm inside the ship, I feel a bit haunted, like something is scratching the inside of my skull, but it just doesn't break out of that prison."

"I know the feeling. It took a lot of work to finally break through my amnesia."

"I do get fleeting images of things, short glimpses, like ghosts at best, but nothing with the clarity that you have."

"Maybe you should let Serena have a go at you?" she adds an impish smirk.

"She offered, I declined."

"Because?"

"Much as I like Serena, I don't fancy letting anyone inside my head. It is already confusing enough."

She raises her glass and clinks his and then they drink.

9

The next morning, they gather with the Prime Minister who is pacing the stony beach, waiting in anticipation. Her face is rippled with a burgeoning worry over the task she faces.

Naturally, her Cabinet members and other military brass, some of whom are standing off to one side, are concerned about how much time the nation's leader is spending in dialogue with an alien entity, even feeling a little left out of the party.

Her secretary approaches her. "Can I get you a cup of tea, ma'am, you're look'n a tad bit stressed."

"Thanks, Nellie, but no." She shakes her head. "I feel like I'm liv'n in Kubrick's film, Clockwork Orange."

"Not familiar with that particular one, I'm afraid."

She fixes a stony on her. "Agh, you Millennials!"

Someone motions her to the lift, where she joins Kaetlyn and Colonel Desmond. She offers a weak smile to Kaetlyn, "Top of the morn to you, lass," she says, and then a curt nod to the Colonel. Otherwise, she is silent as a mannequin as they rise into the air, but her eyes cannot help but notice the flock of media on the nearby cliff, where television cameras are filming their every move.

The novelty that she is about to enter an alien craft and speak to its computer is now overshadowed by the reality facing her – how to stop an impending global disaster.

Once inside the craft, Kaetlyn situates herself on the large chair, as usual. She turns to the PM and nods to the adjacent seat, but Dot declines with a shake of her head. "I prefer to stand, thanks."

Kaetlyn places her hand on the black console and a split second later a three-dimensional face appears.

"Hi L.I.N." begins Kaetlyn, "The PM would like to continue the conversation."

“Hello again, Mrs. Malone,” says L.I.N. “Where shall we begin?”

The PM proceeds with sobriety. “In order for me to be an ambassador on your behalf, so to speak, I need to better understand YOU.”

“And why is that, if I may ask?”

Dot’s lips curl to one side. “Well, for one, you are from another planet.”

“True.”

“And you are not quite like any computer I …”

“Artificial Intelligence is the more appropriate term.”

“Which is why I am inquiring, because the first thing I will be challenged about is the veracity and credibility of the source of information, which is you.”

“There is Kaetlyn too.”

The PM nods with a conciliatory smile at Kaetlyn. “Yes, unfortunately, Ms. O’Sullivan is regarded more as a spectacle at this time, and her circumstances …”

“You mean her reference to her past life aboard this craft?”

“Yes, that, has yet to be accepted by most people in positions of authority as more than …” she pauses, “paranormal for lack of a better word.”

Kaetlyn grins.

“Which it is not,” says L.I.N.

“No, of course not, and anyone who knows her and has had the opportunity to work with her, knows that Kaetlyn is telling the truth, certainly her truth, but the media paints whatever picture it cares to paint, and those in positions of power, with something to protect, are not easily swayed by the words of a nineteen year-old Irish lass who claims to have been the captain of this very vessel, one sent to save us from some existential event at the hands of global warming."

"I understand your rationale, Prime Minister. What questions do you have?"

"What does L.I.N. stand for?"

"L.I.N. is an acronym. In our language, it is differently spelled, but in yours it translates to **Live-Intelligent-Network."**

"Does that mean you are alive or just a replication of something?"

L.I.N. smiles. "Is there a difference?"

A quizzical look catches Dot's face.

L.I.N.'s holographic image suddenly transforms from just her face to her full figure, standing next to the Prime Minister, towering over seven feet tall, an impressive sight with her silver dreadlocks, feminine curves, and eyes as deep and tantalizing as a goddess.

The PM steps back as she looks up at her. "My god, is this actually …"

"Yes, this is the average height of the race who created me, and I, in most respects, represent their features."

"Quite stunning, I must say."

“Thank you. Now, to address this issue of AI. While I am a synthetic, I am aware of being aware, and that, by definition, makes me a living entity. You have cells which constitute your body, whereas I am constituted of digital blocks, like the binary components of computers on your world, but much more advanced, because my matrix draws on quantum dynamics not yet utilized here on Earth.”

“Are you capable of independent decision? I mean, can you do whatever you want?”

“I’d like to think so,” she grins, “but there are limitations built into my coding.”

“You mean, like the laws of robotics?”

“Ahh. A fascinating concept which I recently studied while searching your worldwide web. You are referring to Isaac Asimov’s laws…” she points to a holographic screen which appears and reads.

- *A robot may not injure a human being or, through inaction, allow a human being to come to harm.*
- *A robot must obey the orders given it by human beings except where such orders would conflict with the First Law.*
- *A robot must protect its own existence so long as such protection does not conflict with the First or Second Laws*

"It is my understanding that the primary laws of robotics are there to ensure that AI remains in servitude to its creators."

L.I.N. offers a smile. "I prefer not to see myself as a slave, but if your concern is that I present a threat to other creatures, or that I am capable of independent and hostile acts against you, then rest assured, my programming prohibits such."

"How do you differentiate between right and wrong?"

"A philosophical question, is it not?"

"Not really. We have laws and moral codes, what is your paradigm?"

"My logic extends beyond the moralities of right and wrong or good and bad as you define them. I am the byproduct of countless cultural infusions – spanning entire galaxies. My deductions and by consequence, my actions, are always based on the greatest good – but that is a spectrum that extends far beyond your concept of what is right and what is wrong – because here on Earth, right and wrong are a matter of viewpoint, depending on who it serves."

"Are you capable of destruction?"

"If it is within the parameters of the greatest good, and does not harm my creators, and by corollary, other sentient beings, and if by failing to destroy something would result in greater destruction, then yes, I can independently destroy or even kill something, or someone."

The PM takes a deep breath. Feeling a little more relaxed.

"Ask me your next question, Dot."

"I see a role developing for myself, as an ambassador for the plan you propose to deal with our global warming issue, and as such, I am forced to face certain realities."

"Indeed – and difficult ones too."

"Were you simply talking to me, I would give your plan the green light right now, and I would prepare my nation for what it must face to do our part to reverse the debacle that has begun. However, before speaking to you, I had my doubts. I cannot say that Russia, China, nor even America, or other places, will agree unilaterally to the terms you laid out – and those nations can tip the scale."

Dot walks along one wall, gently sliding her hand across its cool surface as she continues to speak. "In an ideal world, we would call the leaders together, show them the rather sobering facts, brief them on this plan, timetable its implementation, execute a program to educate the general public on what must be done and what to expect, set up contingencies and plans to compensate for food production, energy, etc. all on a scale that defies anything we have ever done before, certainly never as a unified race of people."

"But this is not an ideal world, is it?" chimes L.I.N.

“Far from it,” answers Dot as she stops to look at Kaetlyn and then Desmond. “I assume you’ve already done your own projections on the problems we will face.”

“I have done many models using current circumstances and extrapolating the outcomes for each.”

“And?”

“You are going up against tremendous obstacles, not only the political dynamics, which I consider to be the least of your problems, but in fact, the unseen theater behind the scenes.”

“You’re referring to the industrial, corporate and financial complex– right?”

L.I.N. nods. “Yes. Political entities come and go, but the other establishment remains in power. Those institutions have a great deal to lose in the execution of this plan, and I suspect that those most entrenched in their empires and wealth, will not go along with sanctions required to reduce global CO2 emissions.”

Dot sighs as her eyes idly drift to the portal, looking out at the Celtic Sea, stretching as far as the horizon. She speaks with a dreamy tone. “As a young girl I had this vision that one day I might lead this nation to greater heights. Back then it was just a whim, a whisper of a dream, and now, here I am,” her eyes turn to fix on L.I.N. “After all the parades and the honeymoon was over, and I dug into the job of leading,

I came face-to-face with the rather sobering reality that my station was as temporary as a leaf in the wind, and in many ways, just a figurehead to placate the people and make them think that they had a hand in navigating their futures, and the democracy they believe in. In time, it became evident to me that there were two levels of power not only in my nation, but the world; the governing power, the one the people elected and the lowest of the two by far, and those with the most influencing power, the banks, the financial institutions, the corporate hegemonies, an integrated and complex establishment that goes on, long after political parties disappear from office. I will head this nation for one term, two if I am lucky, but those steering the ship, those who control the wealth, the commerce, the visceral lifeblood, they go on and on and on, and eventually, they are the ones who dictate the terms of the game." She sighs. "What do you recommend I do – how can I win at this and make a difference in terms of saving our world?"

"It is my estimation that the only workable approach will be a hard one; that is, to convince your counterparts to approve unilateral sanctions in the accomplishment of Net-Zero-Emissions and include in those sanctions the wherewithal for governing powers to deal with the hidden oligarchies who will undoubtedly attempt to stop this from happening."

"You mean, throw a hard punch and see what comes back?"

L.I.N. smiles. "There is no way to stop a bully than to bully him back, am I correct?"

"Aye, and where I come from, one good punch puts a bully in his place," answers the Prime Minister.

"Then I suggest you get ready to provoke that fight, because this one will probably take a lot more than one punch."

10 Palo Alto, California

The home of ADX, located in Palo Alto, California, is one of the epicenters of technological development unlike anything else.

The seven-story semi-circular structure faces the San Francisco Bay.

Underground are subterranean layers where the real work is done, new developments which are kept from the eyes of the world at large.

On the face it puts up to the world, ADX specializes in advanced engineered components for use in military aircraft, weaponry, and satellites; however, behind the façade, obscured by veils of secrecy, is the real theater.

Those who work on the highest tier are security rated to a level that makes NSA security protocols nothing in comparison.

Since its inception in 1995, ADX was gifted with information which no other private military contractor possessed. In fact, most Presidents of the United States since the 1950's, including every single top member of present and past Presidential Administrations, had no clue that ADX possessed alien technology which the military the Air Force, had gleaned from several alien crafts recovered over the past seven decades.

ADX had been exclusively tasked to use the off-world material to develop new weapons, including crafts that could replicate the functionality of the alien ships recovered from various crash sites, including those that had been shot down by the Air Force.

Over the years, ADX had produced advanced EMP cannons, capable of directionally neutralizing an entire fleet of ships, or knocking out missiles in flight before they ever reached their targets, or even nullifying the electronics of an advancing army. They had also developed a beta version of a craft that could exceed speeds of any known military plane, moreover, could accomplish maneuvers that were both astounding and violated the very laws of physics. And more.

ADX was referred to, by those knowledgeable in the military community, as Pandora's Box, because in fact, no one quite knew what would come out of that developmental cauldron.

The secrecy surrounding these developments was on the order of life and death, and in fact, the private security force which ADX was authorized to maintain, at a hefty cost, was tasked not only with policing every aspect of the company's activities, but stopping any leaks, by whatever means.

If the American taxpayers knew that their money was being spent keeping one of the greatest secrets of the world from their eyes, while the same governing powers maintained a policy of defusing any credibility about ET, they might not see the upside like those in the military community do.

Rockwell Sims, CEO of ADX, sits at the head of the conference table, a titanic chrome-polished slab of metal alloy that spreads the length of his massive office, appearing more like the deck of an aircraft carrier than anything else.

Staff file into the room and silently take their seats.

Sims, with his usual grim glare, watches on and then, after a moment of uncomfortable silence, fixes his gaze on them.

"Are we ready?"

"Yes," answers the SOO, or Senior Operations Officer.

"We are going to have one shot at this, Mags, and we cannot mess it up. I'm told that President Tamp himself sanctioned the operation."

"I understand," she answers.

Rockwell cues his assistant who taps a computer and brings up an image on a large wall screen for all to see.

Sims stands and slowly circles the deck. “Before I authorize this operation, we need to be sure that no added information has surfaced about those alien crafts.” He raises a brow and looks to another man who sits, waiting, it seems, for his cue to speak.

“The latest news is that the Prime Minister of Ireland interacted with the ship’s computer again,” answers the man.

“And?”

“Irish military is holding their cards close to their chest, but our sources indicate that the Prime Minister is planning to call a Summit of all world leaders to propose what this computer terms the *Intervention*, to deal with global warming.”

Rockwell lets out an indignant huff as he returns to his seat and stares at another screen, livestreaming from one of their satellites, showing the two crafts hovering over the southwest coast of Ireland. He lowers his chin to the palm of his right hand and lets his eyes glide back to the SOO. “Are we absolutely certain the EMP will be enough to start that ship running, and will be undetectable?”

“We’ve tested incremental strengths with Big George,” she begins, in reference to the name given to the EMP cannon, “so we know exactly how much punch it will give. To anyone on site it will appear as nothing more than a small flash."

Rockwell's head lightly bobs. "Assuming the EMP doesn't entirely disable it."

"There is always a chance of that happening, however, we've compared our blast ratio to that which the Irish used to disable the Russian trawler seven weeks ago, when they forced the alien craft to escape from Russian hands. Our blast will match that, but not exceed it."

Rockwell Sims remains silent as he digests it all. Once he greenlights the operation, responsibility for what happens next will be entirely in his hands. His employers, the U.S. military, are paying a high sum for capturing the most valuable piece of alien hardware ever since Roswell in 1947; and of course, complete secrecy and anonymity is necessary. There can be no slightest chance that anyone, under whatever circumstances, can ever prove ADX's complicity in making not just one, but two, alien crafts, currently the object of a global audience, suddenly disappear, a magician's trick of unparalleled precedence.

Sims nods, "Okay, let 'er rip."

11

"So, what happens next?" asks Kaetlyn, a wistful touch to her voice.

Colonel Desmond, the one military man who had been associated with the project since the very beginning when the alien craft had first been discovered embedded in the cliffside nearby, glances through the window of the hut which has been set up within the militarized zone. A subtle sigh escapes his lips.

"It's gonna be a political shite-show now, lass."

A smile creases her lips. It was the answer she expected to hear, feeling the same sentiment herself. "Yeah, figured you'd say that."

Desmond's eyes drifts to hers. "The politicos will talk and argue over this for weeks, maybe months." His head shakes. "It is one of the reasons I went into the military. I despise bureaucracy."

"And meanwhile the icecaps are disappearing so fast that scientists have stopped estimating any time frame. It is just inevitability now."

Desmond's face betrays his fatigue. "I know." He glances back up at the ships in the sky above. "The answer to this fook'n disaster is apparently sitting in those crafts and we're gonna argue about minutiae while Mother Nature kicks are collective arses closer to extinction."

Kaetlyn studies his face for a moment. “Tell me about EMO.”

He turns to fix an eye on her. “How do you know about that?”

She grins. “L.I.N. mentioned it to me after the last talk with the PM.”

“It stands for Emergency Mobilization Operations. Tactical and strategic contingencies designed to mobilize resources on a national level in the event of major disasters.”

“Does that include global warming?”

“Not of this magnitude.”

“And you know that other governments have the same?”

“It is not like we all sit around talking about our EMOs, but we know the Yanks and Ivan have theirs. Don’t know about China or India, I think they’ve got so many people to do deal with that it’s a toss of the cards with them.”

“L.I.N. mentioned this for a reason.”

He nods. “I’d wager she was trying to spotlight the fact that unifying of all nations around a singular plan, might not be so easy.”

“Because they already have their own plans.”

“Right. Which means that Ivan, or China, or others, might not want to play ball with this whole *Intervention* deal. They figure they can just sit it out and wait for the worst to pass.”

"So, the Prime Minister really has her work cut out for her."

Colonel Desmond shakes his head as his eyes drift back to hovering crafts. "Lass, she's headed into a shite-storm of biblical proportions, that's all I know for sure."

12

"You're unusually quiet tonight," says Harry O'Sullivan to his daughter across the dinner table.

Kaetlyn stares at her half-eaten lamb stew, "Lots to think about, dad."

"You're knee deep in the shite, now, lass. I'm impressed you're hold'n it together so well."

Kaetlyn draws a breath to relieve the growing tension inside. A cognitive sense is pounding away at her, like the tremor from a strong wind knocking at the window – heralding a coming storm. Something foreboding is in the air.

The front doorbell rings, yanking her back from a darker place.

Her mother returns with Shamus by her side. "Sit," she commands as she points to the chair next to Kaetlyn, and then proceeds to dish out a helping of stew for him. Even though Shamus has just had dinner, he knows better than to refuse the offering from Ms. O'Sullivan, who takes offense to any refusal of food.

"Mr. O'Sullivan," he nods.

"How are ya, lad?"

"Better than Kaet, I suspect," he answers with a glance her way.

"She's a mite stressed," answers Harry. "You can ease 'er mind a tat."

"I'll try my best."

When dinner is over, Kaet and Shamus put on their winter gear and trudge out into the night. The air is crisp, with a heavy mantle of gray wrapped over the land and a light snow drifting down from the heavens above.

Shamus notes her silence. "What's on your mind?"

Kaetlyn kicks at a mound of snow. "Just worried."

"Bout?"

"I feel like we're in the middle of the perfect storm."

"It's been a damn storm from the day this whole thing started, Kaet."

"Yeah, I know, but no one's made a move since the whole incident up in the North Sea. The Yanks have their ships out there, watching us like hawks; the Russians, dona' know what they are up to; meanwhile, we are procrastinating at best, and the rest of the world is watching this like it is another episode of the

Kardashians. I feel like there is a burning fuse and it is ending soon."

Shamus listens, watching her speak, holding back on talking to her about the subject that hangs between them like an elephant in the room, but which both are avoiding.

Since her near fatal shooting, he has not probed further into their past relationship aboard the craft.

Kaetlyn turns an eye at him. "You have gone quiet on me. Where'd you go?"

He shrugs. "Just think'n 'bout what you said." he pauses, "you should talk to L.I.N. about your concerns."

"Been thinking the same thing. I need to get a private audience with her without everyone else listening in."

"Talk to Desmond about it? He is on your side."

13

Colonel Desmond's eyes remain fixed on a spot on the distant wall as he listens to Kaetlyn. When she finishes, he turns to her with a pensive look on his face.

"That's a big ask, Kaet, considering how much pressure we are all under to get to the bottom of this whole thing."

"I know."

"You are asking me to authorize letting you have a private dialogue with L.I.N., with no one else present. The optics on that will not be good. Is there something you are not telling me, lass?"

Kaetlyn leans closer. "When I was in the coma, something happened."

"What?"

"I went deeper than I could ever have done with Serena during our regressive therapy. I could see my entire past life passing by, like I was sitting in a theater watching it all happen. It was so bizarre, so surreal, and yet, it was me, back then. Scenes from another world, another planet, glimpses of a life lived, and even memories aboard that ship …" she turns to peer through the window of the hut at the craft hovering above and then back to him. "Like any dream, the details are fuzzy, but I know for sure that I was reexperiencing a life I once lived."

"Okay."

"I haven't talked to anyone about it, except Shamus and Serena."

Desmond tips his head. "Why?"

She shrugs. "Because, when I woke up, it felt like I was grasping at dust motes in a storm, it was so confusing. But almost immediately, something started to happen, my past started to come together, like a puzzle, bit by bit. It's not all there yet, but each time I meet with L.I.N., she is the catalyst that speeds up the process of remembering."

"What kind of things are you remembering?"

Kaetlyn's lip curls into a grin. "Well… for instance, I'm pretty sure I could navigate that ship up there?"

Desmond leans back in his chair, pressing a finger to his lips as he ponders her words.

"I see."

"Your reaction is exactly why I haven't said anything to others. You are concerned, aren't you?"

"Well, when you say that you can fly that thing, it does change the perspective."

"Right. And how will others see it if they think I can suddenly take off in it?"

"Not so well, I expect."

Desmond straightens in his chair, a dour aspect clouding his face. He leans closer. "You did the right thing, lass, by keeping this to yourself. If this got out, you would become a target. Right now, people want those ships. You …" he smiles, "if anything, are probably seen as either a means to an end, or an impediment."

"Now you understand my reluctance."

14

Holding a hot cup of tea in one hand and a plate of scones in the other, Serena deftly navigates through a cluster of fold up tables and chairs to where Kaetlyn and Shamus are, and then eases into a chair next to Kaetlyn as a shiver runs through her bones.

"The air in here feels like bloody ice," she comments as she looks around the military hut and tries to suppress the shiver clattering through her.

"Cold as a witch's tit, if ya ask me," chimes Shamus.

Serena raises a brow. "Have you wondered who produced that saying … I mean, how on Earth would anyone really know that a witch's tit is cold?"

Shamus lets out a chuckle. "A stupid question that only a bloody shrink could possibly pose."

Serena laughs at his comment. "Aye, but one that you donna' have an answer to either."

Except for short dialogues, the two have not spoken at length since Kaetlyn's recovery from the shooting. During her comatose state, Shamus had practically slept in the hospital room next to her, during which time Serena had spent hours in dialogue with him.

Although it was no secret to the world at large that Shamus had also been aboard that very craft, with Kaetlyn, in their previous lifetime, his fame was but a shadow next to her, as he had not been able to overcome the amnesia, the mental block between one life and the next, one which Kaetlyn had managed to navigate with amazing lucidity.

Serena had tried to probe Shamus, to see if he could see any light at the end of the same tunnel, but each time they spoke of it, the best he could recall were faint shadows, like specters passing through his fog-ridden mind – and each time she offered her services to him, he declined.

"How you doin'?" she asks him.

"I'm fine," he smiles, "and you?"

"Been keeping busy."

"New patients?"

Serena pinches her lips as her head rocks back and forth. "Nope. I have been asked by Colonel Desmond to keep my timetable clear so that I can remain a groupie to … you know … *Star Girl*," she steals a look at Kaetlyn who hears the comment.

"Stop calling me that," grumbles Kaetlyn.

"Could be worse," responds Shamus.

"Oh, really."

"Yeah, they could be calling you Mork, or Freaky Kaety, or …"

Kaetlyn stops him mid-sentence, "Whatever!"

"What do you hope to accomplish with this private dialogue with L.I.N.?" asks Serena.

Kaetlyn shrugs. "Clarity."

Serena studies her a moment before speaking, "What is it that's really bothering you?"

Kaetlyn turns to her. "I feel like two people trying to occupy the same head."

Shamus tips his head. "Which pretty much violates the laws of physics."

His comment lightens her mood. "Exactly. Two things cannot occupy the same locale."

"But you're not a thing," responds Serena. "This is you in two different theaters, that's all."

"I know that, but … what I'm trying to reconcile is why I'm still resisting who I was, or am … see what I mean," she shakes her head, "it's confusing."

"That's understandable."

"It isn't to me. It's just damn annoying …"

Colonel Desmond enters the hut at that instant – letting a brutally frigid wind in with him. He approaches. "I've fought some tough military engagements in my time, but that crowd…" he casts a disparaging look at the group beyond the window, "they're fook'n tougher than getting inside a witch's panties."

Serena rolls her eyes. "Agh, seriously, titties and panties, again!?"

Colonel Desmond flicks her a confusing look as he turns to Kaetlyn. "You got your private dialogue, lass, but do not count on it happening again. The only contingency is that I must go with you, that was the best I could do."

15 Coast of Ireland

Desmond remains in the anteroom, just outside the main control room of the alien craft, while Kaetlyn continues in, something he agreed he would do for her, but did not mention to the group standing on the shore below.

"Hi Kaetlyn, nice to see you back," says L.I.N. "May I ask, why is Colonel Desmond sitting outside?"

"I wanted a private dialogue."

"I see. Why, if I may ask?"

"While I was in the coma, you know," she touches a finger to the tender spot on the side of her head, "I started to remember things. At first, I thought I was dreaming, even having flashbacks that I heard can happen as one dies, I do not know which, it felt so surreal, but when I woke up, I knew I had crossed over into my former life as the captain of this vessel and mission. And…" she pauses, "ever since that moment I've had more insights, as if a door has been unlocked and the memories are flooding in now."

"I'm very glad to hear that."

Kaetlyn expels a sigh. "It's very confusing to me, to be honest."

"Why?"

"Which is really me? Am I a Black girl who grew up in a small village in Ireland or am I the captain of … this?" she waves her hand about the interior.

"Neither, I suspect," answers L.I.N.

"What do you mean by that?"

"We have not discussed the technical aspects of your experience, and I realize, now that I have studied available material on the subject here on Earth, that it is considered more paranormal than anything, but the fact is that you are an immortal, Kaetlyn – just like every person on this planet. The only difference between you and them, is that most of them don't know it, or at best, only accept it within the framework of what they have been taught to believe by religious doctrine or other authorities … something about the afterlife and heaven and hell and all that," she flicks a dismissive brow.

"I get that, the issue is reconciling the two. It feels like the more I find out about my past life, the more I feel compelled to be that person."

L.I.N. moves closer. "It is not a matter of becoming one or the other, Kaet, it is a matter of acceptance. You are who you are, inside. That does not change lifetime to lifetime based on the different theaters you live in. You are, in my observation, simply refusing to accept the whole package."

Kaetlyn is silent for a time before speaking, "No matter how much I remember about my past," she looks up at L.I.N., "I can't quite get a grip on how to deal with the whole global warming issue and all that is happening now."

"It can appear daunting, but it is certainly not daunting," says L.I.N.

"Easy for you to say, but the whole fook'n world is watching me, as if I'm supposed to save it, or just disappear."

L.I.N. turns to her and for a brief second the look in her eyes suggest a fleeting manifestation of annoyance.

"There is only one way for us to succeed at this, Kaet."

"How?"

"It is time for you to assume your proper role."

"What do you mean?"

"Up until now you have taken small steps in the right direction. Given the circumstances we face, you must now take the leap, take charge of this ship, and stop asking me to do your job as the captain of this mission."

A shocked look sweeps across her face, "Why are you saying that? You could just as easily execute the entire *Intervention* without me?"

“I appreciate the vote of confidence, however, the parameters of this mission, moreover, my programming protocols, prohibit my doing so. And besides, the world is not going to listen to an alien A.I. They will, and are, listening to you, Kaetlyn.”

“What do you mean that your programming prohibits you?”

“I am designed to navigate this ship, to protect it and its crew and contents, to assist in observations, analyses, and planning, but I cannot, under any circumstances, initiate the prime directives of the mission. If that were not the case, then yes, I could have acted by now without involving you, but I cannot.”

“You’re saying that the *Intervention* can’t be executed unless I say so?”

“In so many words, yes.”

“Then I give you carte blanche, go for it.”

“It doesn’t work like that.”

Kaetlyn lets out a frustrating sigh. “How does it work, L.I.N.?”

“I am quite smart and handy to have around. I can independently act on certain contingencies, such as removing this vessel from any area where its well-being is threatened. I can also, in the event of a total mission failure, opt to navigate the ship back to our home world. Within the parameters of my programming, I am flexible, but when it comes to the final decisions, when, where, and how the Intervention is to be done, and then doing it, that requires the captain, or her assigned deputy, and in this case, unfortunately, Shamus is not up to the task – so that leaves you."

She pauses. "When you showed up and announced to me that you had started to remember your former existence as captain of this vessel, it seemed logical to me to stay the course. I have been patiently waiting for you to overcome your mental blocks, Kaetlyn. But now, we are at a threshold. You must either assume full responsibility for this mission once again, and if you do not, nothing further will happen and I will be forced to act on the final contingency and return to our home world, leaving Earth to face its fate."

O

1 Copenhagen

The *Comwell Conference Center Copenhagen*, an ultra-modern facility located near the Copenhagen International Airport, had never hosted a meeting like this one.

Their largest conference facility, equipped with the most advanced audio-visual tech in the world, including their signature *iButler*, a digital conference interface that serviced the guests with everything from fulfilling requests for drinks or snacks, to connecting them with associates across the globe, or even advising on local attractions in Copenhagen, was filled with the world's political leaders – who had flown to Copenhagen to attend this, the most significant meeting ever held. The only nations that declined to attend were North Korea, Venezuela, and Myanmar.

For Dorothy Malone, the Prime Minister of Ireland, certainly not one of the largest nor most influential of the countries represented, it was a defining moment – not to mention completely surreal for her, being the only leader to have parlayed with the alien computer, L.I.N., it was agreed that she should head up the conference.

The last to take their seats, certainly not arriving to the party early, were the Presidents of China, Russia, and the United States – as if by doing so, it was their way of accenting privileged status.

The mood is tense in the hall as they wait for the conference to begin.

Hushed conversations can be heard weaving through the group like a flitting wind.

A hand presses to Dot's shoulder; she turns with a nervous flick in her face, to see her counterpart and friend, the Chancellor of Germany, smiling at her. "You probably have the most captive audience in the world," says the Chancellor.

"Between you and me," whispers the Dot, "I'm piss'n ma pants."

"You'll do fine, just don't let them," she subtly nods to the last three to have taken their seats, "try to intimidate you."

Dot draws a breath to calm her nerves as the doors close and all eyes turn to her.

She begins, "This meeting requires no introduction, so I will dispense with any formalities. I want to remind you that everything that happens here is being streamed live through the media portals to the world. Everything we say and do is being watched by millions, even billions. Many of our military leaders have already met to discuss contingencies with regards to the Visitors, the term generally accepted with reference to the alien ships currently hovering over the coast of my nation, this conference however, has nothing to do with the military, it has to do with our collective responsibility as the governing powers to act in the best interests of the world – and not just our national interests."

She pauses, noting that the faces remain as stoic and unresponsive as statues.

"As you all know, I have had the opportunity of engaging a dialogue with the A.I. computer, known as L.I.N. We have prepared a video presentation so you can watch our short discussions. Nothing has been edited. You will, no doubt, feel a certain sense of surrealism as you watch this presentation, a surrealism that I was challenged to overcome as I sat inside the alien craft, speaking with this A.I, as she … it, detailed the *Intervention*, a plan to save our world from the debacle we now face."

2 Gordon Military Base, Alaska

Draw a line on a map, starting from the Gordon Military Base military base, located on the northern slope of Alaska, bordering the Arctic Ocean and the northwesterly edge of the Canadian Yukon, all the way to Ireland, and it appears like a straight tangent on a two-dimensional map, measuring roughly 5000 kilometers, but in actuality, with the curvature of the Earth factored in, it is further.

The Gordon Military Base is nominally used by the U.S. Airforce as a defensive outpost, but in fact, its real purpose is to provide a secret compound for the military contractor, ADX, to develop and perfect weapons without the eyes of the world snooping on them.

Cal Discher, ADX's Director of Research & Development, along with a small team of his technicians, and a security detail that would challenge the Presidential Secret Service, stand by as the final preparations are made for the launch of the ADX-SR missile.

They could have fired the missile from one of two ADX satellites orbiting the Earth, but the weather conditions over the Irish coast were so horrid and the winter cloud-cover so thick, that they could not afford a hit or miss scenario.

Cal holds the satcom in his hand, gripping it tightly as sweat pours off his forehead.

His nerves are at the breaking point.

Who wouldn't be?! He thinks. What he is about to do will change the course of history. Not to mention the fact that if he messes up, it seems by the grim looking gun bearers standing nearby, that he might be used as target practice.

One just never knows with Rockwell Sims, the CEO of ADX, who has conferred him with the duty of overseeing the operation in its final stage. Sims, he knows all too well, is a ruthless man. The job requires a wolf-like temperament, but his dedication and passion, moreover, his marriage to the US military and their agenda as laid out for ADX, seems to drive him more than eating or breathing – even living.

Cal had joined on several years ago with ADX because of his engineering background and love of developmental tech, and of course, when he was admitted to the inner circle, bonded up to his ass, and it was revealed to him that the source of the technology they were repurposing was off-world in nature, that is, alien, he could hardly have refused the offer.

That relationship came with a price. It was a marriage that could not easily be broken. In fact, senior level employees, like himself, were expected to remain loyal to the end and from what he had heard of the few who had left ADX, the process was grim at best.

He wipes the sweat from his forehead, stealing a look at the stoned-faced guards standing nearby.

"We're ready," announces his lead technician.

Cal leans looks down at the console, studying the telemetry, making sure that every smallest detail is accurate. He could have programmed the launch himself, but Rockwell insisted on having a technical team on site, so that Cal could remain his interface – even, a scapegoat, should anything go awry. Again, this was Rockwell Sims – a man dedicated to himself, first.

He brings the satcom to his lips and presses the button linking him from the edge of the Arctic Circle to Rockwell's comfortable office in sunny California.

"We're ready," he announces with a hushed tone.

"Good!" comes the loud vociferous response. "Let 'er rip," responds Rockwell with the same cavalier tone, as if he were telling him to order an Uber or a pizza.

Cal takes a deep breath, nods at the technician, and watches the video feed showing the missile sitting atop its launch vehicle, as it suddenly jumps into the night sky, like a flare.

The sense that dominates him then, is not pride, nor joy, nor anything positive – it is something else, more like trepidation for his collaboration in what is about to happen thousands of miles away.

3 Southwest Coast of Ireland

Since the arrival of the alien ships, nothing less than a global conflagration had been sparked, with fires burning in countless places and burning stronger by the day.

The fact that no cover up could be done of the obvious fact that two crafts, not of this Earth, were hovering over the coast of Ireland, was causing the very pillars of mediocrity to shake as religious leaders, groups, right down to heads of parishes and even sect leaders, were having countless dialogues, in many nations, about what it meant.

Did their god, in fact, create life elsewhere than on Earth? If so, why was it missing from the narrative they taught and believed?

Was this a sign of the imminent coming of the Apocalypse, where God had abandoned us, leaving humanity to eke out its survival in the face of existential global warming, and now, an alien intervention?

Authorities who propounded existential theories, were now scrambling to review, or rewrite, the narrative.

Advocates of Darwin's Theory of Evolution came under intense fire from all angles, because how was it that sentient species, albeit taller and questionably more aesthetic, existed elsewhere in the galaxy if everything and everyone was the result of a singular spontaneous organic evolution from the primordial seas?

And as to the Big Bang Theory, which claimed that everything was the result of a singular explosion – how was it possible that in the improbable vastness of the Universe that separated us – that similar intelligence, similar physiology, and more, just happened to spark into existence elsewhere from one singularity - the chances being one in a billion – at best?

Authoritative texts were now coming under question in most lands.

Schools of learning were now facing a growing crisis of credibility, as both the faculty and student body, were challenging the veracity of their curriculums.

If the Visitors were real, a fact that could hardly be denied by their continued presence, then how many more civilizations and sentient life forms existed out there?

Moreover, and more to the point, another conflagration of discussions was tidal waving across the globe; how much of this was known about, and how much was hidden from public view, and for that matter, why, and why were we spending so much time, blood and money fighting over scraps of land, when obviously there were other worlds out there in the stars?

Debates and challenges raged across the world like a boreal fire sweeping the continents.

But here, on the lonely stretch of the Irish coast, there was only a feeling of desolation at this time of night, as Sergeant McCoy and his team braced a brutal Celtic wind as they patrolled the area. Despite their winter gear, the cold hand of the wind managed to seep through, forcing them to think of little else than a warm bed when their shift ended.

In addition to the people on his team, electronic sensors, and cameras with night vision, had been set up around the entire perimeter, which would alert to any intruders.

McCoy looks at his watch. *Still three hours before they are relieved*, he thinks as he catches the silhouette of two of his people patrolling the distant extremities.

He stomps his feet to force his blood to circulate and then leans into the radio affixed to his shoulder. "How we doin' lads and lasses."

"Cold as a witch's nipple up here, Sarge," answers the detail high up above on the escarpment.

"Ya wouldn't know what a cold nipple tastes like ya half-witted bodach," comes the response from one of his female crew, followed by the giggles which could be heard rippling over the otherwise silent beachhead.

McCoy grins. "Well, stay alert. Soon we can wrap ourselves under blankets …" but even before he can finish his sentence there comes a reverberation unlike anything he has ever experienced, as if something has just passed through his body with a thousand pinpricks suddenly rippling through him.

A mild terror takes hold as the entire site goes black – as if someone has just flipped a kill switch to every electronic device.

In the distance, a backup generator groans to life, the only device not powered by electricity.

“Units’ 1 and 2, do you have eyes on anything or anyone?”

There is no response.

He presses the button to his radio but there is no response.

McCoy desperately scans the beach for any signs of an incursion but sees nothing.

He turns his gaze upward into the night sky, and to his utter shock, instead of two alien crafts hovering above, there is nothing but empty blackness.

“Fook me!”

4 Copenhagen

A sonorous clang pulls Dot Malone from a cantankerous sleep.

Hotels must be the last place in the world that still use landlines, she thinks irritably as she sluggishly reaches for the receiver on the night table.

“Yes?”

Her assistant answers. “Ma’am, we’ve got a severe problem,” at which she explains the latest news.

Dorothy Malone hangs up, her stomach, already in a state of discontent after spending a day in a meeting with world leaders, discussing the possibility of an extinction event at the hands of Mother Nature, and now this!

She dons her clothes, does a quick fix to her hair, and powders her face to cover her tired visage, and then turns to leave the hotel room when a knock comes. Opening the door, uniformed men face her.

"Prime Minister, we need to escort you to the conference facility at once."

Stepping in stride with the Danish Police Force, who have been tasked to provide security for the conference, she soon arrives at the conference facility where she finds the other attendees being ushered in, looking equally disheveled and distraught at this time of the early morning.

It takes only moments for the room to fill with the somber and dark faces of people, who, like her, have already heard the news.

The Visitors have vanished!

5 Palo Alto, California

Unlike the rest of the world, now riveted and shocked by the news of their disappearance, Rockwell Sims, CEO of ADX, knows exactly what happened to the alien crafts.

"Where are they now," he asks the small team of technicians located at lower levels from his penthouse.

"They're still on the move, sir," answers the lead man.

"Are they slowing at all?"

"No, sir, still moving at over Mach 7."

"*Amazing. Seven times the speed of sound,* he thinks to himself. Let me know when they stop, and where. I need exact coordinates."

He turns to look out at the Golden Gate Bridge in the distance. His mind is on fire with the potentiality, and of course, the pot of gold, at the end of this rainbow once they get hold of those crafts.

"Admiral Greg Willis, of the Joint Chiefs of Staff, is calling on your private line," announces his digital secretary.

Admiral Willis charges into the dialogue. "I hope your guys have this shitstorm under control."

Rockwell grins. "Don't worry, Admiral, we're tracking them as we speak. Once they settle down, we'll move in."

Willis could be heard taking a deep breath. "We better get there first because I'll guarantee you that dozens of satellites are probably trying to find those things."

"And they won't find them."

"Because of the Quantum Plasma that the missile released?"

"Trust the science, Greg. My team examined QP for months – it works, and only we can track those crafts because of it."

Willis expels a nervous breath. "Don't get overly confident, Sims. We're not out of the woods yet, and you still have to get inside those ships once we get them."

"I'm well aware of what's expected of us."

"I'll be meeting with the Joint Chiefs of Staff and the President in an hour, and they'll be expecting some news."

"You'll be the first to know."

6 Copenhagen

After hours spent in heated discussion with other world leaders just the day before, Dorothy Malone finds herself facing an even tougher crowd today.

With the disappearance of the two alien crafts, the dialogue has shifted. Her message to them, or rather, L.I.N.'s message, of how to address the global warming crisis is no longer the pressing issue that it was.

Rarely speaking up, possibly because his English is less than fluent, the Russian President finally stands and cuts the air with the next words, which he delivers in his abrasive native language.

"Эта конференция сейчас бессмысленна. По крайней мере, пока эти инопланетные корабли не найдены, если они не покинули нашу планету."

His translator rapidly follows. ***"My President says that this conference is pointless."***

"We should not assume that, Vlad," begins Dot, but he cuts her off as his voice escalates.

"Позвольте мне быть ясным. Если и когда эти корабли появятся снова, Россия не согласится с этими условиями, установленными этим компьютером ..." he accentuates his words with a dismissive flick of his hand.

The translator speaks. ***"Let me be clear. Even if these ships show up again, Russia will not agree to the terms set by this thing … this computer. It is out of the question..."***

The Russian President continues, *"Мы сделаем все возможное, чтобы сократить выбросы углерода, но думать, что мы снизим углеродный след почти до нуля в течение года или даже двух лет, это безумие и нанесет вред моей нации!"*

"We will do our part to reduce carbon emissions, but to think that we will reduce the carbon footprint to nearly zero within a year or even two years, is insane and would cripple my nation."

With that, he promptly marches from the room.

Dot Malone feels herself sinking into the quagmire as the meeting spirals out of her control.

7 Coast of Ireland

When Kaetlyn arrives at the site and sees no ships hovering above, it leaves her with a strange sense of abandonment – as if she has just lost something visceral, something quintessentially part of her very being.

Over the past days she has tried to reconcile what L.I.N. said to her, *"Take control, become the captain of this mission again, or else ..."*

Those words haunt her now, even more so as she stares into the void above.

If only I had listened to her, none of this would be happening... she thinks as she feels an ominous weight moving in.

Shamus steps next to her and squeezes her arm. "You, okay?"

"This feels like a déjà vu."

"Yeah, it does."

Colonel Desmond approaches. "Any thoughts, lass?"

Kaetlyn's head rocks back and forth.

"Did something happen just before the ships disappeared?" asks Shamus.

"We're pretty sure it was an EMP of some sort."

"How do you know?"

"Every piece of electronic equipment within half a kilometer of this spot, went dead. Short of cutting power device, only an EMP can accomplish that." Desmond shakes his head, clearly upset. "We just can't figure out how it was delivered. None of our satellites or tracking stations detected anything in this airspace."

"So, someone played the same card on us, forcing L.I.N. to initiate evasive maneuvers to protect the ship," says Shamus.

"That is the only reasonable explanation for their sudden disappearance." He turns to Kaetlyn. "Do you think L.I.N. will come back, like she did the last time?"

"In our last talk she said the only reason she is sticking around is because of me."

Desmond raises a brow. "Why? It seems to me that L.I.N. is entirely capable of doing whatever she wants to – even the *Intervention*."

"That is what I thought too until she clarified it. The truth is, she can't do the *Intervention* without me, or …" she looks to Shamus, "him."

"You're telling me that she can't pull this off without you?"

"That's what she said to me and that's why she keeps coming back." Kaetlyn pauses. "Besides her routine protocols, the only contingency she is allowed to act on independent of anyone, is to protect the ship, or, failing our mission, return to our home world."

Desmond's eyes drift to the sea, spotting the blinking lights of the American naval ships in the distance. "This just keeps getting better," he says with a sigh.

"You think it was them, the Yanks?" asks Shamus.

Desmond shrugs. "We'll see, won't we. If they pull their fleet in the next day or two, that would be the smoking gun – wouldn't it?"

8 Palo Alto, California

Rockwell Sims feels the gentle nudge to his arm. He rolls over from a light sleep and opens his eyes to see his secretary smiling at him. "What is it?"

She hands him his phone.

"Yes?"

"Sir," begins the technician, "they landed."

Rockwell surges from his office sofa, straightens his tie and hair, and sets off for the fifth floor. When he arrives, the technicians assigned the task of tracking the alien ships look up at him with expectant eyes.

"Where?"

The lead techie points to the screen, "Southwest of Whitehorse in the Yukon."

"What's the terrain like?"

"Extremely mountainous," answers another.

"Fucking, Canada," the words hush from Rockwell's mouth. "Deploy the recovery team."

9 Russia

On the most northerly tip of Severny Island, located just four hundred kilometers north of the Russian mainland, sits a Russian geological station.

It is the final outpost in an otherwise bleak and barren Arctic domain.

Gregor Alexeev has been stationed there for two years – with only intermittent breaks to visit his family on the mainland. The 58-year-old is also a native of the region, having grown up on the mainland to the south.

As he sits there, staring out into the white void of the brutally cold terrain, his thoughts drift back to the story his grandfather once told him, of a time when the Russian military arrived at their village on Severny, and force-evacuated all the inhabitants to the mainland. Little was said as to why, just that it was all part of protecting the Motherland, and in the space of two weeks, after hundreds of inhabitants had been uprooted and planted hundreds of kilometers to the south, the truth outed – not because anyone told them, but because, one day, the sky lit up like a bright light bulb as the tremors shook their temporary wood shakes.

It was an event that shocked not only his people, but the world, as the Russian military announced the detonation of the ***Tsar Bomba***, on October 30th, 1961; the most powerful nuclear weapon ever tested on Earth, a singular anthropogenic explosion that spread more pollutants than any other bomb exploded in known human history, yielding 50 megatons of TNT, which was scaled down from its maximum 100 megaton design-yield.

Ever since then, few, if any people have repopulated the region, although there still exists a military base on the island.

Situated at his outpost, Gregor sometimes feels like he is sitting on the dark side of the moon. So far from civilization, so remote from anything, he is forced to deal with his sense of disenfranchisement by sometimes imagining himself as the last surviving man in the world – and with that, he plays out a train of scenarios in his mind to help cope with his severe isolation.

Gregor had volunteered for the post, driven by a sense of affinity for the land of his forebearers, and moreover, a passion to protect its natural beauty and the fact that the terrain was changing in ways that most people were either not aware of, or did not care to have the spotlight cast on. Although he reported the facts routinely in his briefs which he sent to the senior-most geological scientists in Moscow, it seemed as if nothing was ever made public about the fact that over the past nineteen months alone, he had measured a 33% increase in the rate of melt of the ice cap upon which his very station rested.

Two years ago, when he first arrived here, it was estimated that forty percent of the island was covered by the Severny ice cap, the largest glacial area, by volume, in Europe.

In his short tenure at the station, those figures were rapidly shifting.

Glacial melt had reached an all-time high. In fact, the terrain he had become so accustomed to seeing every day and night, had visually shifted over time, and it seemed as if the horizon was lower, and it was.

The ice was simply disappearing.

There were times when his station experienced what amounted to the rumblings of an ice-quake, the equivalent of an earthquake, but in this case, it was the shifting of the very ice cap he stood on.

The signs were clear – and he reported it as factually as he could – global warming was diminishing the Arctic at an alarming rate.

If the Russian authorities who received his information were alarmed as he was, they certainly did not show it, nor did they make the facts known to the rest of the world, which of course was not particularly surprising considering the massive monetary interests which the Russian government and its corporate affiliates, had in developing mineral and oil resources in the Arctic.

No one wanted to draw unnecessary attention to the greenhouse element because everyone was more interested in bleeding the resources dry and making as much money as possible.

In fact, for those leveraging the Arctic resources for financial gain, the optics were entirely different. Melting icecaps was a godsend because it reduced the cost of mining its resources.

Gregor raises his binoculars to scan the horizon. Barren as it is, it has a mesmerizing beauty to it – the combination of immense white, the glacial formations that are sculped by Nature, the intensely blue sky by day and depthless black by night, and then of course the lights – the polar lights, also called the northern lights or the aurora borealis.

Desolate, yet magical.

He moves his binoculars with incremental precision, viewing the distant waters, the meeting point between the Barents Sea to his left, the Kara Sea to his right, and straight ahead, far ahead, the Arctic Ocean.

His eye catches the shape of something sitting on a promontory. Out here, any discrepancy in the white landscape shows up with ease.

A Polar Bear sits in the open.

Beautiful creatures, he muses aloud – even though there is no one else to hear his commentary.

The bear's attention seems fixed on something. He lowers his binoculars and scans the nearby inlet, and there, pressing against the edge of an ice floe, are two ships – whalers, bobbing in the sea like plastic jugs, their sides scratching against the ice, something no Captain in his or her right mind, would ever permit.

An odd feeling permeates his bones. *That cannot be right.*

Donning his winter gear, he checks his high-powered rifle, his emergency kit, and his radio, and then steps out into the maws of the Arctic.

Kicking his winter sled into action, he hops aboard and slowly eases the throttle, letting the machine glide across the terrain in the direction of the ships. As he nears them, the sound of his engine spooks the bear. It takes off, loping across the ice in the other direction.

As he draws near, he sees what he could not from a distance. The side of each ship, grated and pounded by the ice, is severely damaged – in high waters, they would surely sink.

“Hello!” he yells, but there is no answer.

He steps to the very tip of the ice and manages to grab onto a mooring line dangling idly over the side of one ship.

Scaling the ice is no easy task, but as he slips over the rail and drops to the deck, the sight he sees stops him dead in his tracks.

10 Canada

The RCMP station, located on the southwest tip of Banks Island, just outside the small village of Sachs Harbour in the Inuvik Region, with a population of only 103 people, is the most northerly Canadian policing force in the second largest land mass in the world.

While providing law and order for the tiny village, the station’s prime agenda is to serve as a watchdog in coordination with Canadian military, helping to track the coming and going of ships passing through the Beaufort Sea and Arctic Ocean near the Canadian border.

“Sir,” his voice cuts through the light chatter emanating from a nearby radio channel.

Sergeant McCalin steps across the room. “What is it Simmons?” he asks of his fellow RCMP officer.

Simmons points to his radar screen, showing an unusual blotch, a composite of individual spots nearby.

The sergeant stares at the strange cluster. "What's your take on it?"

"By their size and shape, I'd say they're ships for sure, but it makes no sense that they are clustered together like that, they should be distanced apart, especially in these waters."

"How far from here?"

"Roughly nine kilometers south-south-west of us."

"Can we chance the skiff or is the ice too thick."

Simmons shrugs. "The channel is still open, but we would have to be back before nightfall when all hell freezes over.

Within minutes the two are geared up and board the small patrol boat docked nearby. Its powerful twin engines cut into the frigid waters of the Beaufort as they take off.

It takes fifteen minutes, navigating between ice floes, to reach the coordinates.

Sergeant McCalin cuts the engines, letting them drift silently toward the sight.

Like driftwood floating aimlessly in the sea, four fishing vessels, two of them flying Canadian colors, another flying the American flag, and the fourth, a Russian trawler, are clustered together, so close that they can hear the grating of metal against metal as the sea rocks the ships into one another.

It is an eerie and haunting discordance – one that does not belong in this domain.

McCalin guns the engine, moving closer to one of the vessels. “Go up on that one,” he points to the portside of a small whaler sitting low in the water.

Simmons scales the side, lands on the aft deck and is met with the same disconcerting silence. It feels lifeless and its entire deck is layered with ice.

A chill consumes him, not the chill of the Arctic, it is something else – something ominous.

He approaches a hatch, manages to open it after kicking and cracking the ice sealing its edges, and then lowers himself into the dark gangway.

A putrid smell accosts him, causing a reflexive gagging sensation.

Covering his mouth, he flashes his light into what appears to be the galley, and instantly, the beam reveals a grotesque theater of bodies, like frozen mannequins, scattered about.

Some are drooped over the table, some are sitting upright with their heads askew, as if frozen on the spot, others lie in fetal positions on the floor; but on every face is written the last moments of their lives, scribed in letters of anguish, with blood caked lips and pools of red frozen around them.

11 Finland

Bikká has been driving all night.

She is heading home, to Inari, not only a popular destination for tourists, located in the far north of Finland, but also the cultural center for the Sami people – her people.

Her parents still live in the same modest one-story *talo*, Finnish for *house*, that she was born and raised in, before heading off to start her career as a virologist, where she now works as a senior researcher in the city of Kemi, to the south.

The short vacation will afford her time to see family and friends, while organizing her thoughts around the next phase of her career. She has been studying, and now, working with the field for eight years, and is considered one of the nation's top virologists.

Always on the search for new strains, new vaccines, and even new threats to world health, Bikká's passion for the subject has been rewarded in the knowledge that she has saved lives, even though she spends most of her time hunkering over vials of goop, peering into electronic scopes, testing, retesting, on and on for the pot of gold somewhere at the end of each research project.

The E75 traverses some of the most stunning, and yet, remote country in the world, with a thick wall of tall firs standing like an endless column of soldiers on each side of the road, heavily laden with a mantle of snow and ice.

As the morning sun creeps over the tree line, a welcoming sign appears, both in Sami and English, on behalf of the visitors to this part of Finland, announcing that she is just minutes from her family home.

Tired, from a long drive, she looks forward to seeing the happy faces of her mother and father, both now retired, and both growing rounder and more wrinkled by the year.

Her twin brother, Olavi, works as a chemist in the local paper mill, and her younger sister is celebrating her eighteenth birthday on this very day, one of the reasons for the visit.

As she approaches the town center, something odd catches her eye.

At first, she assumes it must be a dead reindeer lying to one side of the road, but then her eyes see what her mind refused to initially accept. She slams on the brakes and skids to a stop.

Exiting the vehicle, she stares down at the body, bloated with red blotchy skin and eyes which press out of their sockets, like small balls. Blood, seeping from the mouth and nostrils, is freakishly frozen in strands – like drops that never quite made it to the ground to join the puddle of such.

"*What the …*" she begins when her eye catches another sight.

She approaches, and gasps at the sight of three children, their faces etched with agony as they grip their throats – their skin wracked with red welts and blood streaming from their lips.

Panic sets in as she starts to realize what she must be looking at; she knows the signs from her extensive training in the field – only a virus could do such a thing to people.

She races back to her car, flips open the trunk and immediately dons a hazmat suit, one she always keeps on hand for her studies and work at the virology institute in Kemi.

Back in her car, she speeds down the road, fearing the worst and the worst is more than any nightmare she could ever have envisioned as she passes through streets where bodies are scattered about, the horror of their deaths painted on their faces as the final legacy of their existence.

Moments later she enters her home, filled with consternation at what she will find.

Tears spill from her eyes, clouding her vision through the mask covering her face as she looks down at the bodies of her mother and father, holding hands, their corpses bloated and red, their eyes nearly popping, and near to them, stretched out on the sofa, her sister.

She slumps to the floor as the agony shreds her soul.

12

With the sudden exit of the Russian President and his convoy, Dorothy Malone finds herself facing a brewing storm of discontent.

"May I please have your attention," she says, repeating it twice before the heated discussions subside. "Thank you. I realize this turn of events has changed the circumstances of our meeting; however, it does not change the fact that we are still facing an imminent debacle which we must come to terms with, with or without the help of …" she pauses, "the Visitors."

The Brazilian President, who had recently taken office in the wake of her disastrous predecessor, a man who permitted the Amazon to be raped and burned at an alarming rate, speaks up. "I agree. Whether this alien intervention will happen at this point is irrelevant to the fact that we are facing a crisis." She pauses. "And please, make no mistake about it, I am quite aware of the contribution my predecessors have made to this debacle. My government stands ready to assist, in whatever way we can."

Dot feels a slight sense of relief – someone has finally taken a positive step forward.

The Lithuanian leader enters the discussion. "Despite the radical proposal from this, alien computer," a sardonic grin creases his lips, "it seems to me that its rationale is solid, and that we must reduce carbon emissions on an urgent basis?"

The Prime Minister of New Zealand speaks up, "I am prepared to offer a plan to my nation to move toward Net-Zero carbon emissions."

Dot is about to respond when a single voice cuts the air. She turns to the woman, Canada's first female Prime Minister. "Yes, Lisbeth – what is it?"

The Canadian PM is pale as she nods at her computer. "I've just received a very alarming report from the Commissioner of the RCMP," she begins. The room quiets. "Twenty-one fishing trawlers and two of our RCMP cutters, have been found afloat in the Arctic region of Canada."

"What do you mean, afloat?" asks President Tamp of the United States, who has sat in relative silence up until now.

Lisbeth turns an eye to him. "Every soul on those vessels was dead."

Shocked looks take over.

"Dead! Of what?" he asks.

Lisbeth tips an eye at the report and then back to them. "An RCMP team, on site, is suggesting it is probably a virus of some kind – but that is yet to be verified."

She reads more of the report. "RCMP units also checked two nearby Inuit villages along the north-west coast of the Yukon and found all of its inhabitants dead. The symptoms are the same as those found on the ships."

"How many people are we talking about?" asks Dot of her counterpart.

The Canadian PM looks up from the computer, her face now ashen, as if all the life has been suddenly sucked from her. "834, so far."

13 The Arctic

Cal Discher watches on as the CH-53K King Stallion transport helicopter, the largest in the US military arsenal, and certainly the largest of its kind in the world, with a payload capacity of sixteen tons, descends with its prize, the smaller of the two alien crafts, secured by steel cables wrapped around it.

Despite the arctic winds, the pilot deftly eases the object onto a mobile platform and then a team moves in, disengaging the cables, and with a thumbs up, the chopper heads off for the second, larger craft, which is being guarded in a mountainous valley seventy-five kilometers away.

The head of the recovery team approaches Cal with a smile pasted to his lips. "Well, there she is," he announces with a flick of his head. "Over to you and your think-tank boys."

"How long before the second craft is here," asks Cal.

The man shrugs. "If the weather holds up, figure on four to five hours. It is bigger and heavier than this one."

"And what about the Canadian authorities. I am told they noticed our presence there?"

The man smirks and spits. "Don't worry about the Canucks. My men have that site locked down tighter than a camel's ass. We'll be out of there before they come snooping."

Cal does not particularly share the man's confidence or arrogance, but he is not about to get into an argument with a man holding a gun.

With tepid steps, he approaches the craft. Its sleek obsidian surface is mesmerizing to look at. As he walks around it, thoroughly inspecting as he does, not a single seam is visible on the entire surface, as if it had been poured from a single mold.

He runs his hand along its cool smooth surface, feeling as he does, like he is violating the work of a famously dead artist, one that he and the others have just stolen from the world.

A member of his team approaches, "Should we give it another shot from Big George, just to make sure that computer doesn't wake up?" asks the man, referring to the portable EMP cannon.

Cal shakes his head. "No. Get it inside the hangar first. I want to avoid using too much EMP as the surge might damage the computer … L.I.N. Just make sure people are staffing the EMPs in the event we have to use it again."

Cal watches as they roll the craft into the hangar.

A cold, brutally freezing wind, smacks into him, almost knocking him over, as if an omen of something that is coming.

He tries to shake away the feeling, but try as he does, he cannot shake the ominous feeling that hangs over him.

14

Haulbowline, an island south of Cork, Ireland, and home to the Irish Naval Service and its headquarters, has suddenly become the center of the universe for Kaetlyn as two-armed military personnel escort her from the helicopter to a four-story structure, and then directly to a large conference facility on the top floor.

Seated at a long table are people dressed in both military and civilian garb.

The air is thick with a sense of foreboding.

Colonel Desmond motions her to a seat next to him as a woman in civilian clothes pauses her talk to the group and waits for her to be seated.

Kaetlyn has no idea why she is there, nor even, who these people are, but there is no mistaking the fact that something important is happening.

Resuming her talk, the woman points to a map of the Arctic region and draws a laser pointer across it, stretching from the Aleutians all the way around the polar cap and back to the very tip of the Eastern Siberian peninsula. "Each red marker you see here is a confirmed site where the infection has been detected so far."

Kaetlyn feels even more confused at what she is seeing. All she knows is that the Colonel had called her hours ago, informing her that he had arranged a transport to bring her there.

Desmond leans in and whispers. "I will explain soon. Just listen for now."

"As you can see," continues the speaker, who is one of three top pathologists in Ireland, "the permeation is spreading at an alarming rate, and already, we have reports of 87 settlements along the coastal region between Canada and Russia alone, where thousands have been found dead, manifesting the same symptoms as those found on the ships in that region."

"Has anyone established the source?" asks someone.

The woman points to an island in the Arctic Circle, north of the Russian mainland. "In fact, yes. The Severny Island, its northern region, is a massive ice cap, one of the largest in the world. The first report received by Russian authorities came from a geologist stationed at a remote outpost there. He reported ships adrift in the nearby Barents Sea. His report, along with one received from a Canadian outpost, is what set off the alarm bells. When a Russian team arrived on site this morning, to investigate the Severny situation, they found the geologist dead, but their initial investigation suggested two things. First, their readings when compared to others now taken across the Arctic, showed the highest concentration of the pathogen, literally .009 percent permeation, compared to .003 percent elsewhere, suggesting that the source of the virus seems to be coming from that very ice cap. Secondly, they deduced, although this is theoretical at this point, that the only logical explanation for such a high concentration in that precise area, must be connected to the melting of the ice cap."

"Come again," asks a senior military official.

Another image flashes up on the screen. "This is a diagram showing the layering of the icecap in that region based on geological surveys performed over the years by Russian mining and oil conglomerates. In fact, the very man who reported this incident, has also been reporting the on-going declination of that area." She points. "The first layer of the ice cap is what you see with the eyes, but beneath that is a foundation of ice which some geologists suggest has been frozen, and untouched, for tens or even hundreds of millions of years. The Russian scientists on site have a theory that the melting ice cap has released a viral pathogen that existed millions of years ago, maybe as part of the Jurassic Epoch, maybe as a result of an extinction event that wiped out most living things in the wake of the Ice Age, possibly even a meteor that crashed there eons ago; but whatever it is, something seems to have been unleashed from that ice, and that pathogen is killing everything in its path, both human and animal."

"How does it attack the body – do we know?" asks another.

"Initial autopsies show that the pathogen attacks the lungs. The victims experience great difficulty breathing because of internal swelling and hemorrhaging, followed by agonizing pain as the lungs fill with blood and fluids. Death follows swiftly." She clicks the remote bringing up images of bodies, a sight that causes a collective gasp. "It is not pretty, I know. Besides the internal damage to the lungs, this virus results in these red welts on the skin, like open lesions. This could be the virus permeating the body and finally exiting through the skin. We do not know yet. The blood seeping through the mouth and nostrils is uniform in all cases, coming up from the lungs as they choke to death."

The room is silent and solemn.

"Is it airborne?" asks Colonel Desmond, intentionally breaking the taciturnity.

"That would be the most likely means of permeation," she answers, "and the only explanation for its rapid spread across that region."

"How likely is it to spread southward?" asks another civilian.

"This entire region," she passes her laser across the Arctic belt, "is a high-pressure zone, and if we are lucky, it will help contain the virus long enough for us to study it and determine a handling. However, that said, it is likely that an airborne virus will inevitably find its way southward, sooner than later."

The silence is broken by hushed dialogue.

The Admiral of the Irish fleet stands. "Thank you, Dr. Minnis. Now, what we must discuss are contingency plans to deal with this, since, as we all know, our nation's location makes it very vulnerable."

Desmond nods to the Admiral who tacitly gives him leave as he nudges Kaetlyn from the room and takes her to the nearby Officer's lounge, sits her down and then lowers himself in a chair across from her. "Sorry, I didn't have time to prepare you for that, lass."

Kaetlyn is still trying to reconcile what it all means.

"What is this virus?"

"What you just heard is only known about by a handful of people in different nations. We have made a pact between us all, even the Russians, to try and contain it as much as possible to prevent global panic, but it is just a matter of time before it leaks to the media and world knows." He looks around the room, making sure no one is within earshot, and then turns back to her. "I wanted you to hear about this first-hand, because it appears to have everything to do with global warming." He offers a tremulous smile. "The real reason I called you here, lass, is because we received a communique from Canadian Military Intelligence, which included these satellite images."

She cocks her head as she studies the grainy shots. "Is that our ships?"

"One of their satellites picked up two strange objects in a mountainous region bordering Alaska and the Yukon. A secondary satellite, passing over the same region some hours later, detected a lot of activity around those objects, and a third fly-by six hours later, showed nothing there."

Kaetlyn's brow edges upward. "You think it was the ships?"

"We do. The telemetry matches their dimensions. The Canadians agree, which is why they contacted us. In fact, one of their weather satellites spotted a large military transport flying between an American military base on the coast of Alaska, and that mountainous region where the objects were first spotted."

"Very large as in …?

"It's since been confirmed as a CH-53K King Stallion – the largest military transport helicopter in the American fleet. That vehicle is capable of carrying a payload as heavy as the first craft, possibly even the second one."

"So, you think the Americans found the ships and took them to their base in Alaska?"

"Unless someone hijacked one of the most expensive helicopters in the world, it seems logical to assume that the US military is playing a hidden card."

"Okay …?" she tips her head. "The punchline, please…"

"You told me that you might be able to navigate that ship – remember?"

"I did."

"Could you do it even without L.I.N.'s help?"

Kaetlyn pauses. "I'd prefer not to – but it really depends on the condition of the ship."

"I'm pretty sure we can assume the Yanks used an EMP to disable L.I.N."

She leans closer. “You are seriously considering taking it back from them? Has anyone even tried talking to the Yanks?”

Desmond shakes his head. “Do you really think they are going to admit to having just stolen those two crafts? We are past diplomatic negotiations, Kaet. The Americans are acting out of self-interest. They will not play ball with us if it means letting those crafts out of their hands for even a second.”

“Okay, but even if I do succeed in flying that ship out of there, what does that have to do with this virus.”

“I don’t know yet, but I do know this – we’re going to need all the help we can get to stop this virus.”

“And if we fail?” asks Kaetlyn with a heavy visage.

“Then, we’ll need a miracle because as far as I can tell, the Apocalypse is coming.”

15

As dim traces of her digital consciousness start to spark to life again, L.I.N. muses for the space of a nanosecond about her existence. She is aware that this is the third time that her functionality has been temporarily disabled by an external force; and although she does not feel upset about it, in the conventional sense, she is cognizant of something bordering on frustration, that her existence can so easily be shut off.

As her digital synapses start up again, a quick analysis, taking just micro-seconds at best, confirms her circumstances. The initial blast which had initiated her emergency protocol, had come from above, an intense energy pulse which had prompted her to invoke the contingency mandate to protect the ship and its crew – at which she had instantly removed the ship from its position over the coast, and the drone, which is paired to her, followed, being no more than a servile robot. After landing the ship in the mountainous region, with the drone settling nearby, she started to analyze the situation. It was not long after that a second surge, more powerful than the first, struck the ship and rendered her "unconscious" – for lack of a better term.

She scans the perimeter and sees that she, the ship, is sitting inside a large structure with bright lights shinning down, and moreover, a small group of humans, none of whom she recognizes, who are hovering around the ship with weapons aimed right at her.

She deduces that to remain any longer would constitute an existential threat.

L.I.N. powers up the ship, preparing to escape this place, when another blast permeates her matrix, and as before, everything goes black.

16

Cal Discher stands around a small table with other members of his team, studying the computer mockup of the alien ship, one which his people have prepared using digitally enhanced imaging.

The head of the special security detail enters the room, with a wide grin and interrupts their discussion. “We just nailed that thing again,” he announces.

All heads turn to face him. “What do you mean?” inquires Cal.

“It started to fire up. The computer woke up after the last juice we pumped into it. Anyhow, we shut ‘er down with another dose from Big George,” he proudly announces as he hefts one of the mobile EMP cannons.

Cal bites his tongue, wanting to lecture the trigger-happy jarhead that too much electro-magnetic pulse can permanently damage or destroy the mind of that ship, and it is the mind they are after, the entity called L.I.N., but he represses the urge.

"Thank you for the update," he says as he turns back to the others and says in a hushed voice. "We need to get inside that thing before they fry its circuitry."

One of his team members points to the midsection of the ship. "There," he traces his finger, "is the portal that this girl…"

"Kaetlyn O'Sullivan," interjects Cal.

"Yes, her, this is where she entered the ship each time. I would say that is the most vulnerable point and given that we already know from her descriptions of the ship, and videos taken by those who went in with her, that there is an antechamber there, intended to protect the ship and its crew from pathogens or the like. If we focus our laser on this section alone, it should not compromise the rest of the ship or damage anything vital."

Cal studies the computer graphic, spinning the image with a flick of his finger.

A troubling thought has taken hold, gripping his mind for hours now, something that no one else has voiced or seems even mildly concerned about; the fact this craft belongs to someone, another race, somewhere out there in the stars – and they are about to dissect it without asking their permission.

Do they even know the ship is here, he wonders?

How could they not, considering the technology, moreover, the fact of L.I.N. who must have been in touch with them.

He restrains a shudder, trying not to show his trepidation to the others, while maintaining a good face, because that is what leaders do – put up their best face- right?

"Okay, set up the laser," he nods at his lead engineer.

17

When the Prime Minister of Ireland steps from the plane at the Dublin International Airport on her return from the failed Summit in Copenhagen, not only is there a detail of security personnel waiting to escort her to a car, but the very person whom she dreads meeting is standing there with a dour aspect.

She slips inside the car as does her health minister.

Dot draws a deep breath, already feeling a sense of growing panic in her stomach. "So, Katherine, I assume the forecast is not rosy."

"No, ma'am" answers the woman with a somber tone as she taps her iPad and turns it for her to see. “The red markers are locations where the virus has already been detected.”

Dot stares at the map of Ireland with repressed shock. Markers now reside over Malin Head, Dunegard and Crega, three remote locations on the northerly tip of the nation.

“Detected … how?” she asks, although she senses that the question is rhetorical at best.

The Health Minister’s face darkens even more. “We have 330 confirmed deaths with the same symptoms. I’ve already dispatched teams to the region to start analyzing the virus and its permeation.”

Dot exhales as something dark starts to consume her very soul. “Are we sure it’s the same virus and not just a severe flu outbreak?”

“No, but we’ve never seen a flu that killed so indiscriminately and so absolute, and...” she pauses, “that is 330 humans – the animal figure is easily ten times that amount. There are reports of dead birds everywhere, carcasses of dogs, cats, and other wild animals, all with the same symptoms.”

“Oh my god…” Dot exclaims as a disturbing shudder cut through her like a sharp knife. “If it’s spreading that fast, it must be airborne.”

“Yes, ma’am.”

Dot taps her mobile phone and calls her assistant. “Ruth, call an emergency meeting. I want every cabinet member there when I arrive in thirty minutes.”

18

Admiral, Greg Willis, one of five members of the Joint Chiefs of Staff, a committee composed of heads of each branch of the US military, and himself the top man over the Air Force, sits in his office in one corner of the Pentagon, ironically, the very section of the building which was "reportedly" struck by American Airlines flight 77, with 58 passengers aboard, in the wake of the 9/11 attack.

It never ceases to amuse him as he looks out his window at the White House in the distance, because he knows the truth of what really happened on that day in 2001.

There was no plane that struck the Pentagon. In fact, he was sitting in a meeting two floors down – and the only thing that struck the Pentagon was the news of the debacle unfolding in New York City.

The very idea that a passenger jet could crash into the center of Washington, is and was preposterous. Protocol, in the event of any potential threat to the nation, and especially Washington, mandated that fighter jets out of three air force bases in Maryland and Virginia, would be scrambled and in the air within minutes, patrolling the airspace over the nation's Capital the instant that the first of the Twin Towers had been struck. Had any plane, domestic or otherwise, come anywhere perilously close to the nation's Capital, it would have been shot down long before it ever reached the Capital, let alone the Pentagon. The very fact that the story was bought, emboldened those who had created the narrative, who went on to script the war fever that George Bush, then President, announced as the precursor to an American invasion of Afghanistan.

As he progressed up the ranks, he was admitted to the inner circle and the truth, that the "supposed attack" on 9/11 was nothing more than a ruse intended to garner support, both within the Nation and internationally, for putting American boots on the ground in Afghanistan and establishing a beachhead for American interests there and eventually in Iraq and Iran, and by doing so, preempting another invasion by Russia, which they had attempted in the 1980s.

He smiles, reveling in the fact that so many minds, not only here in America, but around the world, can so easily be swayed by a complete falsehood, an attack that never happened, and given enough media coverage and endorsement from the White House, anyone countering the "fact" was either labelled delusional or a conspiracist. In fact, they expected the conspiracists to grandstand the issue, because the best way to gaslight the public, was to have the naysayers get up on their soapboxes and make unbelievable claims that the United States government conspired to killing over three thousand American civilians just to leverage public opinion and support.

His cell phone vibrates. "Progress?" he answers.

"What the hell is this news I'm hearing about some virus in the Arctic?"

Willis leans forward, speaking more quietly. "What have you heard?"

Sims replies. "You really underestimate me, don't you, Admiral? I have connections in places that even you do not, and they are telling me there's an outbreak of some kind along the Arctic Circle."

"Calm down, Sims. We've got teams up there checking it out."

"When were you planning on telling me that my people might be at risk?"

Willis lets a demonic chuckle escape his throat. "Seriously, Sims, when did you ever give a fuck about "your people." Anyhow, if there is any indication that this virus is coming their way, I will let you know, and we'll arrange an evac team to move them and those ships to another base."

When he hangs up the line, Willis taps the intercom. "Get the Secretary of Health on the line."

A moment later the line buzzes. "Sally, what's the prognosis with this virus?" he asks.

"I just came from a briefing with the President," she begins, "it is bad Greg, really bad. Up until yesterday, the infections and deaths were only detected along the Canadian and Russian fronts, further east, but now we are getting reports from hospitals and clinics, with people showing up with the same symptoms, and worse, deaths, in Point Lay and Wainwright, on the northwestern tip of Alaska."

"Shit!" responds Willis, thinking to himself that the military base where the ADX team is currently working, is clearly in the path of this virus."

"Any idea how fast it's moving?"

"Honestly, we don't know enough about it yet. If it is an airborne virus, then it is a throw of the dice. It could take days or weeks before it starts showing up in the lower hemispheres."

19 Dublin

Following the emergency council, Malcolm Calhoon, the Chief of Staff of the *Irish Defense Forces*, remains behind to speak to the PM in private.

"Prime Minister, I would like to suggest a different approach to this crisis, if I may."

The Vice Admiral waits as the Prime Ministers, also the Supreme Commander of the IDF, and his superior, turns to fix her gaze on him. "Why didn't you bring this up in the meeting just now," she asks.

He tips his head. "It is a delicate matter to discuss in a group setting."

"I see. Then, tell me."

"While I agree, empathetically speaking, with everyone's concerns, and with the idea of sending our forces to these northerly counties to begin evacuations, wouldn't it be more prudent to concentrate resources on Belfast and Dublin, the very hearts of our nation, where the bulk of Irish folk reside, and try to set up a means of maximizing their survival…" he pauses, "assuming that this virus continues its southward assault."

Dot draws a breath. "Are you suggesting we abandon the other areas?"

"No, I am merely suggesting that we focus the bulk of our resources on areas with the densest population. If this virus advances faster than it is, we will not have time to get to every village and town." He pauses with crimped lips. "I know it sounds calloused of me to say this, but we only have so many resources, and it is best to optimize them. We will, of course, deploy teams to Londonderry and surrounding counties, but I believe, in the interests of preventing total panic and total economic collapse, that we send no less than 80% of our forces to Belfast and Dublin, forthwith."

Dot turns to the minister of health who sits nearby busily tapping into a computer. "What do you think, Katherine?"

"I tend to agree with the Vice Admiral's proposal on the simple premise that we can aggregate resources to those two centers, mobilizing hospitals, emergency medical and hazmat supplies, and of course, assuming we can find an antivirus, the most expedient means of saving the most people in the shortest period of time."

"There is another factor to be faced," begins Calhoon, "evacuation. If this becomes a pandemic, we cannot evacuate every living soul from every region, but we can aggregate resources and make Belfast and Dublin the staging points to move people elsewhere."

Dots stares at the large map of Ireland which hangs nearby, her eyes fixing on the small town of Strabane in the northwest corner, right in the path of the advancing virus. She had grown up there. Her family still lived there.

She nods with a sigh. "Do it. And …" she pauses to turn to her press secretary, "there is no point in keeping people in mystery. Prepare a statement for me, announcing a nationwide state of emergency, say exactly why, but not more than what we know, with instructions for people to stay home while we mobilize our teams."

20

Kaetlyn's first response to Colonel Desmond's suggestion that she be part of a covert ops to recover the ship from the American base in Alaska, comes without hesitation, "Of course, I'm in, but I want Shamus and Serena with me."

Desmond's brows narrow. "This is dangerous enough for you ..."

She cuts him off, "I understand the downside, Colonel. But I want them with me."

Colonel Desmond is under no delusion that he can dissuade the headstrong girl. It is not the first time she has dug her heels in and resisted more authoritative brass than him. "As you wish, but…" he is about to say when his Adjutant steps into the room.

"Sir!" the man salutes with a serious demeanor painted on his face.

"What is it, Thompson?"

The Adjutant glances at Kaetlyn and back to the Colonel.

"Say your piece Sergeant, she needs to know whatever it is."

"We've just received a report from the WHO…"

"The World Health Organization?"

"Aye, sir. It has been confirmed that the virus has moved laterally across the entire Alaskan region. If's officially a pandemic now."

"Which means it's headed for that American base?"

"Aye."

Desmond looks turns to Kaetlyn. "Well, lass, the stakes just went up. Still want to be part of this?"

21 Alaska

Cal stands a good distance from the alien craft as his team focuses the most powerful laser ever developed into the side of the alien craft; in fact, the laser was engineered by ADX, yet another of its secret developments.

The air sizzles as the bean kisses the craft, but beyond that, nothing happens. There is no smoke, no acrid smell of burning metal – nothing.

It defies their collective credulity that any substance can resist a weapon-grade laser as powerful as this one – and yet, it does.

"Shut it off!" he commands as he approaches the craft and carefully inspects the hull and carefully runs his hands over the surface where the laser had made contact.

"Unbelievable! It is cool to the touch, and not a mark, not even a scorch," he utters with a shake of his head, thinking of Rockwell Sim's last words to him, still banging in his head like a hammer against the inside of his skull. "*Get inside that thing, Cal. Just do it!"*

Cal approaches the lead technician – feeling a sense of growing desperation as he tries to figure out what to do. "What if we tried several lasers on one spot?"

The man shrugs. "We can give it a go," he says with a sense of dread in his voice.

"You don't sound very confident."

The man turns to Cal with tired eyes. "To be honest, I do not think it's going to work. We've already pumped enough juice into that thing to cut through fifty cars in a matter of seconds, and it isn't making a scratch."

Just then the head of the security team approaches, his weapon casually perched on his shoulder like a baseball bat, as he strides their way. "We've got a problem," he announces.

Cal turns to him. "What?"

"Couple of my guys working the perimeter found some bodies."

"What do you mean bodies?" asks Cal with a shocked look.

The man shrugs. “Locals, you know, Indians or Inuits, whatever they’re called, two men and a kid, floating face down in the water.” He continues.

“An accident?”

The man shakes his head. “No. I saw the bodies. Their skin was bloated like a balloon and covered in red patches.”

It suddenly occurs to Cal that Rockwell Sims is not telling him everything.

22

When the door closes, the PM turns to the Chief of Staff of the *Irish Defense Forces*. “Why wasn’t I informed of this operation in the planning stages, Malcolm? And why are you bringing it to me now, when clearly, you are already moving ahead with it?”

The PM’s nerves were frayed, and that also meant that her temper was on a short fuse.

She waits, grim-faced, for the man to answer.

“The fact of the matter, ma’am, is that everything has moved so fast, and details had to be confirmed, before I could bring it to you.”

She draws a breath to calm her emotions. “Go on.”

He stiffens his back before continuing. "At this point I must enter a waiver in my defense, because quite frankly, this whole matter with the alien crafts, the so-called Visitors, and this whole story with Kaetlyn O'Sullivan and her past life, has not exactly met well with my conservative middle-of-the road view of the world. Nonetheless, our extraordinary situation ..."

Dot cuts him off. "Just get to the point, Malcolm, I'm tired, and frankly, nothing would shock me right now."

"Recent information has given us an opportunity to take back the alien crafts."

"Take back?" she exclaims.

"Late last night, we received satellite footage from our friends in Canadian military intelligence, showing what appears to have been the largest of America's transport helicopters, moving two large objects from a mountainous region in the Yukon, to an American base on the coast of the Arctic. Based on our analysis of those satellite images, we are sure those were the alien crafts."

"The Yanks took them!!?" she utters with sincere surprise.

The man nods.

Dot is momentarily puzzled. "But, why? Why would they pull such a stunt and now?"

Malcolm clasps his hands as he leans closer. "You will recall that less than two months ago, the

Americans dispatched their northern fleet to intercept a Russian trawler with the alien craft aboard it, which was steaming toward Russian domain. That confrontation between the Yanks and Ivan nearly escalated into war. So …" he pauses, "I would not put this past them. They desperately want that craft, and they feel entitled to take it."

"Okay, all that aside, what do you mean by taking them back?"

"We're proposing a joint task force with our special ops units and the Canadians, to secure that base and then fly those ships out?"

Dot raises a brow. "Fly? What are you saying, Malcolm?"

"Ma'am, Kaetlyn O'Sullivan recently divulged to Colonel Desmond that she remembers how to pilot that ship." He pauses with a look of incredulity. "Again, my incredulity aside, that gives us a window of opportunity. We would detain the small military detail and security force at that base, get Kaetlyn into the ship and let her navigate it away to safety, back in orbit. We know the drone will probably follow it since it seems to be in the control of this computer."

Dot ponders for a time. "Why Alaska?"

"Reconnaissance from our friends in Canada suggests that this location is only nominally used for military purposes. Its real purpose is serving as a testing ground for a military contractor called, ADX, which engineers advanced weaponry for the U.S.

military. Their operation is very secretive. The point I am trying to make is that we would not be intruding on a military base, so much as a research facility."

The PM's face blanches. "It's still American turf."

"Aye, ma'am, it is."

"You're seriously considering taking a nineteen-year-old girl on a covert-ops that could turn into a war zone."

The Vice Admiral circles the office before turning to face her. "The Canadian intel is solid, ma'am. That base is currently minimally staffed. A small detail of military personnel and other private security that recently arrived with the alien crafts. We would be going up against, at best, twenty armed personnel."

She tips her head at him. "And what repercussions can we expect?"

"The Americans will be upset, no doubt, but given the circumstances, and the little stunt they just pulled, what can they say or do? We would be holding all the aces and they know it, because if we exposed what they did, they would be overrun with recriminations from the rest of the world."

"But we don't know their full intentions," responds the PM.

Malcolm smiles. "Ma'am, I have absolutely no doubt that President Tamp sanctioned all of this, because to the Yanks, those two ships represent a game changer, an opportunity to make America the premiere military power in the world – and that is a status he would do most anything to achieve – especially if it can win him another term in office."

"The man is self-serving," she muses.

The Vice-Admiral sits across from her. "Why do think the Yanks, or even the Russians, were willing to go to such extremes, practically starting a war over these alien crafts?"

"The technology, of course."

"Precisely. No one knows what is in that ship, or what that computer can tell us, but we do know this, when Desmond's team first found that ship buried in the side of that cliff, it was surrounded by solid rock – which took our team days to excavate."

"I remember that."

He nods and continues, "Kaetlyn O'Sullivan, in her talks with the ship's computer, questioned her about this very fact, and it turns out that this ship possesses a means of transmutation."

The PM raises a questioning brow. "Transmutation?"

"It means it can shift solid rock into something else, making it possible to hide itself in that escarpment for nearly two decades." He pauses. "Imagine what that technology alone would do to our world? Not to mention the fact that whatever that ship is composed of, it is entirely impervious to any forces we have used to cut into it. Imagine what we could do with that material alone? Its value would be inestimable both militarily and commercially."

"I understand all of that, Malcolm, but what does any of this have to do with the virus?"

"Some people on the other side of the fence, over in Russia, scientists and engineers, have offered up a rather bold plan."

"Which is?"

"If we can recover the alien ships, we get L.I.N., or Kaetlyn, whichever, to help us use this technology on transmutation to slow the leakage of the virus."

"How would we do that?"

"The Russian teams on site on Severny, suggested a plan to use drones, with special sensors, to locate the prime areas where the virus is leaking most intensely, and then attempt to plug up the fissures."

"Like plugging up a dam?"

He nods.

"And you think this technology of transmutation, can help?"

"We do not know for sure, but if you consider the sheer magnitude of that icecap, the job of capping off fissures over such a broad area, and how to even do that in a reasonable time, is overwhelming. But, just maybe, this alien computer, L.I.N., can help us with that."

Dot's eyes light up as she realizes the potential. "So, if we can at least slow the leak, even though the melting ice caps will probably continue to release the virus, we buy ourselves time."

"We can save a shite-load of lives."

"And you don't think that bringing this to the attention of the Americans and asking them to cooperate with this plan, will work?"

His face sobers. "Madame Prime Minister, I am a military strategist, not a political one, and I can assure you, nevertheless, given the circumstances, that President Tamp will never let that ship out of their sights." He draws a deep breath. "I have many good friends in the American military hierarchies. Most are good people, with good intentions. Unfortunately, the man at the top of that pyramid, and a handful of others who bow to him, see only one pot of gold, and that is the one that puts America first. Moreover, President Tamp has made his position clear on the matter of global warming – he thinks it is more fake news than anything."

His eyes drift to framed map of Ireland. "And to be frank, the Yanks stand to lose much less than us if this pandemic hits. We are in the path of that coming storm. America has a huge land mass, Canada, which will take the brunt of that virus long before it reaches them." He pauses. "For us, it is a matter of days, a week, before the virus blows southward. We just do not have time to ask for their permission. Millions, maybe even billions of lives are at stake, and I think the risks of getting those ships back is more than justified."

Dot's head bobs. "Alright. Do it!"

23

Shamus sits in silence as the echo of Kaetlyn's words resound in his head.

Across from him sits Serena. Her face is pale and expressionless, like a pool of still milk.

Kaetlyn waits anxiously for a response from either.

"Well, that's a kick in the balls," he finally answers. "But, all things considered, it can't be any worse than the last time we died in that ship," he grins.

Kaetlyn offers a reserved smile and turns to Serena.

Serena shakes her head. "You do realize that I am your damn therapist, right, not your comrade in arms?" She pauses. "And while I appreciate the opportunity to be in the spotlight of the world, why exactly do you want me to put my life in danger?"

Kaetlyn clasps her hand and squeezes it. "I know, it's asking a lot, but you two monkeys have been my anchors through all of this."

"Ahh, so you do need your shrink after all," she says with a smirk.

"Don't let it go to your head … but … yeah, I'd feel a lot better if you were there with me."

Serena rolls her eyes. "So, best-case scenario, we fly out of there alive. Worst-case scenario, the Yanks shoot us before we get inside, or they cart us off to prison, or, because your driving license has expired, we end up crashing in that thing - which means we have about a 33% chance of surviving this whole plan."

"Sounds 'bout right to me," intercedes Shamus.

Serena shakes her head. "I had this silly notion that my life would be kind of normal, you know, help traumatized people, eventually find a suitable Irish lad, have a family, live a nice life, travel, but no…." she looks to Kaetlyn, "I'm a groupie for StarGirl."

Kaetlyn raises a brow, "I'll take that as a yes?"

When the three finally emerge from the small room where Colonel Desmond had left them, the look in Kaetlyn's eyes confirms what he needs to know.

He points. "You'll be wearing those pretty much throughout the mission."

"So, we don't know how far this virus has spread?" asks Serena.

"No."

A sardonic grin creeps across her lips. "This just keeps getting better."

"When do we leave?" asks Kaetlyn as she grabs the nearest suit.

Desmond glances at his watch. "Wheels up in twenty-three minutes."

"No time to say goodbye, I guess," says Shamus.

Desmond meets his eyes. "If we do this right, you'll be home tomorrow sometime."

"Or not," replies Shamus.

Desmond leads them from the building to a large hangar where a plane is being fueled.

He points, "This is an *A320 Airbus* – it'll take us to a Canadian military base near the Arctic circle and from there, we'll switch to a Canadian military transport helicopter which will drop us near the American military base."

"So, the Canadians are in on this too?" asked Shamus.

Desmond nods. "Oh yes, the Yanks dropped the gauntlet on Canada when they pulled that little stunt on Canadian territory. Believe me, the Canucks are pissed."

24

The shock of seeing her family dead, and disfigured with red blotchy skin, as if they had been whipped to death, left Bikká with an overwhelming sense of grief and incipient dread.

She cannot exactly remove her mask to wipe away the tears that spilled, but as her outpouring subsides, she is forced to repress her emotions, because whatever this is, whatever scourge has just wiped out an entire community, could be heading elsewhere.

Stepping outside she walks up the street to nearby houses – friends of the family, people she has known since she was a child.

The carnage is everywhere. People have dropped dead in their tracks with the same symptoms. The frozen blood caked to their lips, horrid as it is, suggests profuse internal bleeding leading to a quick but painful death.

The carcasses of animals, dogs and cats, and scores of birds, litter the landscape like an apocalyptic film.

She photographs everything on her mobile and then gets back inside her car as another emotional surge takes over. When the tears subside, she heads directly to the paper mill where her brother, Olavi, works.

The mill, normally a hub of activity, is as silent as morgue. Carefully stepping around the bodies of workers who had collapsed, she studies them for a moment, their faces tell the story of their last moments of life, all of which suggests that the virus attacked with brutality and speed, even before they had a chance to get medical help.

Inside the mill, the scene is the same, people, scattered about in fetal positions, others died clawing at their throats, others who simply collapsed, blood spilling from their open mouths, blotched and bloated skin, and of course, the deathly silence that fills the air.

A sound catches her attention, like something scraping against a door. She follows it to a room marked with a sign - TOXIC MATERIALS. Peering through a small glass window she sees someone hunched over on their knees, their head hung to the floor.

She tries desperately to open the door, but it does not budge.

The person inside suddenly looks up and through the mask she sees his face. "Olavi!" she screams so loud that it echoes inside her gear.

He points to his oxygen tank. "I need oxygen," he gasps as he slumps to his hands – hanging there as the final seconds of his life ebb away.

She turns and sees a large red button on the wall nearby. She smacks it and the door snaps open. As she races in, she grabs his faltering body, hearing his breathing coming in desperately short haggard gasps.

“Olavi, where is the oxygen stored?” she asks as her eyes work the room.

He raises a wavering hand and points to a cabinet outside the room.

Bikká races to it, opens the doors and finds extra cannisters of oxygen. It takes her a minute to swap out his old tank with a fresh one. He lunges at the air, like a man who has not breathed for minutes.

He finally looks up her, his face pallid and wet, and manages a tepid smile, “What took you so long”?

She wraps her arms around him as tears spill from her eyes. “Oh my god, I thought I had lost you too.”

“What the hell going on, Bikká,” he asks as his eyes suddenly catch the sight of a body lying in a twisted mass nearby.

“Come,” says Bikká, leading him from the carnage, where they can sit.

“A viral outbreak of some kind, that’s all I know.”

“What?!”

“I know the signs, Olavi – and I’ve never seen anything like this before.”

“Is everyone …”

She nods. “I have not found a single person alive, anywhere. They are all dead, Olavi.”

He turns to her, his eyes wide with shock. “All?”

“I was home.”

Tears pool in his eyes.

“Mama and pappa, and ...”

“No, not little sister.”

She waits until his tears subside before asking the question on her mind. “Why did you have a hazmat suit on?”

“It’s standard procedure when we work with toxic material in that room.”

“But why didn’t you take it off?”

“The power went out, and when it does, the door has an automatic locking mechanism to prevent people from getting in. There is supposed to be a back-up generator that kicks in in the event of a power failure, but it did not come on, so I was locked inside, and I did not want to be exposed to the toxic fumes while I was trapped there. I must have banged on that door for hours. I was about to give up hope when you showed up.”

For a moment they are silent as Bikká takes stock of their situation.

“I need your help, Olavi, and I need you to stay objective. You are going to see a lot of death out there, and it is not pretty. We need to gather information and get it back to the Center for Disease Control in Helsinki, and fast.”

His eyes graze over a dead body nearby. “He was my friend. He has a wife and three kids,” he sighs. “And mamma and pappa and …” his eyes water yet again.

“I know.”

“What do you need me to do?”

“Take your friend, there,” she points to the dead man, “put him on that table, and meanwhile I will get my kit from the car. We’re going to assess this virus and see what we can learn about it.”

Olavi turns to her. “Did you have your hazmat suit on when you got here?”

Bikká’s head shakes. “No.”

“Why are you still alive?”

“I don’t know, Olavi. I have been asking myself that question too.”

25

Kaetlyn sits in complete silence during the flight from the Irish Defense Base in Cork to the Canadian military outpost at the furthest outreach of the Yukon Territory.

The trip takes them across the tip of Greenland and along the Arctic circle.

From her vantage point, everything seems so white and pure, but she knows that people are dying by the droves and that a beast of its own is now advancing on humanity.

Something dances in her head, a specter from her past that stabs her already wounded soul, summoning the sense of guilt that if she had accomplished her mission, none of this would be happening now.

She sighs.

Colonel Desmond approaches. He smiles at her. "You okay, lass?"

"As well as can be expected under the circumstances," she answers with forced grin.

He points down at the icy domain. "See that cove up ahead?"

She follows his finger.

"That is where the American base is located. We land in about six minutes. From there, the Canadian military will fly us to within half a kilometer of that base."

"Can't wait."

Desmond fixes a firm eye on her. "I wish I had something wise to say, but I don't, lass."

"It's okay, Colonel. I'm gett'n used to it."

"Indeed, you are," he says as he leaves.

Kaetlyn leans back in her chair and buckles up just as Shamus plunks down next to her.

"So …" he begins with a look of mischief in his eyes. "… you ready for your first test flight in nineteen years?"

"Seriously, I'm not looking forward to it."

For a moment he is silent before he speaks. "You nervous?"

"Piss'n ma pants. You?"

"I was kind of excited about it, but now …" his eyes glance out the window, "that we're almost there I'm feel'n a little less of that."

She squeezes his arm. "Thanks for coming. It means a lot to me."

"After everything we've been through together, I certainly couldn't decline an invitation like this one," he finishes with a lopsided smile.

Kaetlyn turns to the window, her stomach suddenly knotting up as the landing strip, a mere thread of black asphalt in a sea of white, appears ahead.

26

Cal Discher represses a grimace as the pain stabs his chest, yet again.

It feels like countless needles are pricking the inside of his lungs, and the pain is like nothing he has ever experienced in his life.

He watches as two more of the base's military personnel are carried off on stretchers to the sick bay. By his count, there are now four men and two women lying in that room with similar symptoms.

He assumed, at first, that it was a bad flu going around, but now, with the sickly feeling and growing dread inside, it dawns on him that something far worse is going on. Moreover, that his boss, Rockwell Sims, is not telling him everything – which is par for the course for the man, who can be counted on to act in his self-interests, first – others being expendable commodities at best.

He approaches his lead engineer. "That's it, shut it all down."

The man, himself looking pale, responds. "What! Why?"

Cal points to sick bay in the distance. "Something is going on, and it does not feel right. Get everyone aboard the transport, now. We're getting out of here," commands Cal as he heads off to locate the pilot and meanwhile radios his boss, to inform him of his decision.

It takes only minutes before ADX's head of security walks belligerently toward Cal. "What the fuck are you doing?"

"I am shutting it down. Look around you, some of these people are coughing up blood." He looks back at the man. "And, if you haven't noticed, you're looking pallid too."

"I'm fine," he asserts, "and besides, I haven't received any orders to abandon the op."

"I don't care about the operation anymore. I care about these people. I am letting Rockwell know of my decision."

The security man grimaces as he crunches his jaw. "My orders are to make sure nothing interferes with this...."

Cal cuts him off. "Fuck your orders. We are getting on that transport. If you have a problem with that, you can shoot us all."

Cal turns and walks away, trying not to show the pain now gripping him.

27

Two CH-47 Chinooks scudded over the icy terrain at a low altitude to avoid detection, churning up a cloud of surface snow as they pass.

Desmond motions to Kaetlyn, Shamus and Serena, to come closer. "We land in thirty seconds," he announces over the thunderous din of the powerful twin rotary blades.

"You stay behind Duffy and his team," he points to the man. "I'll be heading up the other team. We will secure the perimeter first. When Duffy gives you the green light, you follow him and his men to the craft. Got it?"

All three nod in unison.

"And," he points to the small green light on the chest of his hazmat suit, "if that starts blinking yellow, you let someone know so we can get a new oxygen tank to you. Clear?"

A red lamp suddenly flashes ominously inside the chopper.

"That's our cue!" says Desmond with a wink as he pulls his weapon close to his chest.

The ground comes up fast, meeting the wheels with an impact that jars them to the bone. As the ramp lowers to the ground, a brutal Arctic wind screams into the chopper as if to challenge their very presence.

"Go!" says Desmond as he and his team disappear into the swirl of wind and snow.

Moments pass, and it seems forever as they wait inside the chopper, crouched together. There are no shots. There is nothing but the howl of an angry wind and the bite of frigid air which still, somehow, reminds them that their suits might save them from the virus, but the hand of Old Man Arctic would still win this battle of ultimate survival.

"Team 2," Desmond's voice breaks the silence."

"Go," answers Duffy.

"Bring 'em in, Duff."

With Duffy in the lead and his team flanking the three, they sprint across the open tarmac – in as much as trying to run with hazmat suits feels more like wadding through thick mud. Arriving inside the hangar they see Colonel Desmond and his team staring at something. As they approach, their eyes grow wide with shock. Bodies are scattered around the hangar, bloated corpses with scarlet welts on their skin and blood seeping from their mouths and nostrils, the pain and agony of their decisive moments etched in their faces, as if carved into stone.

"What the fook?!!" exclaims Duffy.

"The virus got 'em," responds Desmond as he turns to the man. "Get them to that ship, Duff," he points to the alien crafts sitting in the center of the hangar. Kaet, you get inside that thing, now. That is an order."

Kaetlyn forces the bile back down her throat as she turns from the grotesque scene.

Seconds later they reach the ship. Kaetlyn steps up to the portal, reaches a hand upward and suddenly realizes that without taking off her gloves, protecting her from the infectious virus, that she cannot tap in the code.

"Fook!" she exclaims as she turns to Shamus. "I can't code in without taking off my glove."

"You can't do that, Kaet," he implores.

"But …" she is about to answer when a shot rings out, pinging off the side of the alien craft so close to her head that it sends Kaetlyn to the ground as terror fills her.

Duffy and his men instinctively form a circle around the three as two more shots slam into the craft.

Colonel Desmond, hearing the concussions, orders his team to scatter in the direction of the shots.

Kaetlyn lies prone on the floor less than a meter from the portal.

Her eyes flick nervously from the craft to the other side of the massive hangar, searching for the source of the shots.

By this time, Desmond and his men have made it to the far end of the hangar, creeping incrementally closer to a small room, with an open door, and there they see the nozzle of a rifle protruding through a broken window, and the shooter, lying on a gurney with his gun tight to his shoulder.

Desmond presses a button on his suit, opening his comm system so he can be heard. "Whoever you are, whatever you think you are doing, please stop. We are the Irish military."

Seconds pass before his weak voice responds. "I don't care if you're Russian, you better leave, or my next shot will kill someone."

"What's your name?" asks Desmond as he motions his men to move closer.

"Doesn't matter. I will be a corpse like the rest of 'em, soon enough" he says, followed by a fit of dreadful coughing that ends with a painful groan.

Desmond uses that brief window and motions his men to storm the room.

The man, the last remaining person alive at the base, looks up at the guns now aimed at him.

"Fuck," he says with a wheeze and another groan of agony, as red spittle flows from the edge of his mouth, and then, he slumps over dead.

"The shooter is dead, Duff," announces Desmond as he approaches them.

"What's the problem, lass?"

"I can't code in unless I can touch the portal with my hand."

Desmond shakes his head as his eyes drift to a body nearby. "I can't let you do that?"

"It's my choice, Colonel. I came here to get those ships…"

Desmond barks back. "No! I am not letting you expose yourself to that virus."

One of his men points to something. "Sir," he nods to a device set on a tripod a distance away.

"What do you make of that, Duff?" asks Desmond.

Duffy, a veteran soldier, and engineer with the corps, walks over and studies it before answering. "I would say it emits an electromagnetic force."

"How can you tell?"

Duffy points to the tip, an extended section with perforations along its surface. "This is not engineered to discharge a projectile or anything solid for that matter, and it doesn't have a channel for a laser. I'd say it emits a pulse, my guess, an EMP."

"Fook!" exclaims Desmond. "They're using these to keep the ship disabled until they get inside."

"Which means that we have no way of knowing how long it will take for L.I.N. to come back online. They caused irreparable damage to her," retorts Kaetlyn.

Surprisingly, the voice that responded is that of Shamus. "No, an EMP pulse would not shut L.I.N. down completely."

Everyone turns to him.

"And you know this, how?" challenges Duffy.

Shamus steals a glance at Kaetlyn who raises an inquiring brow. "I know I've been in the grandstands all this time, but you forget that I was the ship's engineer, aboard that craft, when the Yanks shot us down."

"And what, you're suddenly having an epiphany?" says the man.

Shamus shrugs. "It suddenly occurred to me as you were talking, that L.I.N. has an integrated back-up system that is protected by firewalls and extra defensive walls, so, short of destroying the entire ship, she will eventually come back on-line."

"You're seriously just remembering this now?" asks Colonel Desmond with a tip of his head.

Shamus feels abashed about his assertion, because, like Kaetlyn, the cognitive sense comes from another time and place – in fact, another life. He nods, "Do you really think the designers of that ship were not aware of the disruptive effects of electro-magnetic forces out there," he points to the sky, "when flying ships between entire solar systems where there are solar flares, black holes, and electromagnet storms that make this," he nods at the device on the tripod, "seem like a mere drop in the ocean?"

Desmond smiles. "Fair enough, lad, but the question remains, how long before this back-up system kicks in, because I'm thinking we don't have a lot of time before …"

His sentence is clipped by the sound of an airplane engine cutting through the desolate ambience of the Arctic domain.

Collectively, they run to the opening of the hangar, and watch as two military transports drop from a cloud-scudded sky, hitting the asphalt with an angry slap and churning up a cloud of black smoke as the braking system screeches both planes to an abrupt halt.

As the back ramps deploy, armed personnel pour out onto the tarmac.

"Shit!" utters Desmond.

28 Finland

Bikká ends the call on her mobile and then turns to Olavi.

"That didn't sound good," he says.

"No," she shakes her head. "That was the Director of CDC in Helsinki."

"And?"

Bikká expels a deep breath, causing her hazmat to fog up. "It's officially a pandemic."

"How far has it spread?"

"They've already recorded thousands of deaths along the entire Arctic ring, and it's moving progressively southward."

"Paska!" he exclaims, Finnish for *shit*. "So, what now?"

"The Director was very interested in knowing why I'm still alive."

"Any theories on that?"

"We have been trying different vaccines for the last two years down in Kemi. I could have been exposed to one or more of them, or any combination, but that exposure would have been pretty minimal considering the safety precautions we take." She shrugs with frustration written on her face. “The Director wants me in Helsinki now. They are going to take blood samples from me and see if they can determine what combination, out of probably fifty or more vaccines we’ve been playing with, is the one that saved my ass.”

“If we leave now, we can be in Helsinki by tomorrow morning,” he says. “Not sure if our oxygen will hold up though.”

Her head wags. “We are not driving. A helicopter should be here in less than thirty minutes.”

29

Dorothy Malone sits in the morbid taciturnity of her office, a room that remains as stoic and timeworn as the title it has housed. In fact, the very chair she sits in has been occupied by no less than twenty-eight Prime Ministers before her.

The oak wainscot that skirts the walls, even the wallpaper, bespeaks of both the artisanship that went into its design, and its antiquity.

Even the air seems old and musty, reminiscent of ages gone by.

She sighs as she stares out the window at the city of Dublin.

She loves her country, and loves serving it, but now, it feels as if she is as helpless as the Captain of the Titanic as his ship sinks into sea.

Even though she did not request it, and never would have, her subordinates had organized a rescue operation to the small town in the north, evacuating 330 residents who lived there, including her mom and dad. It was only hours later when the Center for Disease Control's team on the ground reported the first signs of the virus in that very region.

She had just read the most recent reports from teams on the ground, with lucid images not only of the corpses of dead people, but that of thousands of cattle, horses, sheep, dogs, cats and animals of all sorts, even heaps of birds, littering the landscape, all with the same symptoms – bloated and scared corpses - found lying in a pools of their own blood.

A knock jolts her back to the present, "Come in."

Her secretary enters. "Ma'am, the Joint Chief of Staff is on the line for you."

Dot turns to the intercom and presses the button. "Yes, Malcolm."

"It's not good news, ma'am."

She sighs. "I wasn't expecting any, so...tell me."

"We have just received reports of cases in Bangor, just outside of Belfast. The Brits have similar reports from the Isle of Man, Edinburgh, and Glasgow."

"So, it's moving faster than we expected."

"I am afraid so. Do we have the green light to start the evacuation process in Belfast and Dublin?"

Dot draws in a deep breath. "Yes."

"Thank you…"

"Wait! Is there any word from Colonel Desmond's team?" she asks.

"No ma'am."

When the call ends, she slumps back in her chair, thinking to herself that there is no manual for how to deal with something like this.

30

Men charge the hangar, firing off a volley of shots as they do.

It is every bit a battle zone now.

Duffy signals his team to return fire – forcing the American units to hit the asphalt.

Both sides are avoiding kill shots, but because lead is lead, and kills indiscriminately, it is only a matter of time before blood is spilled.

"How many are there?" asks Desmond over the comm.

"Fifteen or so, sir," answers Duffy as he fires off more rounds.

"Avoid kill shots," replies Desmond. "But keep them pinned down."

Desmond turns to Kaetlyn who hovers nearby. "We need to figure out to get you inside without compromising you."

Kaetlyn huffs. "I think that ship has already sailed."

Shamus edges up to where Kaetlyn stands. "Do you have your mobile on you?"

She taps her pocket. "Why?"

"Remember, couple months back when you first made contact with L.I.N?"

"Yeah, so?"

"You didn't do it with the code, not the first time, remember?"

Kaetlyn's eyes light up. "Oh my god, you're right. She cloned herself with my phone. Why didn't I think of that?"

The sound of bullets pinging inside the hangar is becoming terrifyingly tangible.

"Can't hold them much longer," announces Duffy to Desmond.

Desmond turns to Kaetlyn with a desperate look in his face. "It's kind of now or never, lass," he says as he turns and levels his weapon on the hangar doors.

Kaetlyn pulls her mobile phone from the pocket of her hazmat suit and places it flat against the portal, exactly where she normally enters the code.

"Sir," comes the flustered voice of Duffy. "They are going to break through our defensive line any second now. Unless we start a blood bath, I cannot hold 'em any longer."

"Retreat, Duff, get your men the hell out of there," orders Desmond as he hunches down and motions his team to do the same, preparing to defend Kaetlyn and the others at any cost.

Just then, Kaetlyn's mobile lights up like a Christmas tree and the entry hushes open with barely a whisper.

"We're in," she screams to Desmond, as the three disappear inside the craft.

31

The head of the American assault team orders his men to disarm the Irish units, while the rest of his team surround the alien craft.

"Which one of you is in charge?"

Colonel Desmond steps forward. "I am."

"Your name?"

Colonel Patrick Desmond of the Irish Naval Service.

"Well, Colonel, you and your people are in a shitload of trouble." He eyes the craft. "Where are the others?"

"What others?"

The man steps closer. "Don't play games with me, Colonel. You came here to get those things," he nods at the ships, "so, where is the girl?"

"They're inside," casually answers Desmond.

"Tell them to come out, now."

Desmond shrugs. "I have no way of doing that. We can't communicate to them, and we can't get in."

A sneer presses itself to his face as he turns and cues his men who station themselves behind the three EMP cannons triangulated around the craft. "On my mark," he commands, but before he can say another word, a series of shots stops him dead. He turns to see a group charging into the facility with weapons trained on him and his men.

"Drop your weapons, now, or we will shoot," comes the voice.

At that instant, both crafts spur to life with a high-pitched whine, and as everyone watches, they rise into the air, and together, spear through the hangar doors and disappear into the clouds.

Colonel Desmond sighs with relief as a figure approaches him.

“Are you Desmond?” asks the woman through her hazmat.

“I am.”

“Nice to meet you, Colonel.” She extends a gloved hand. “I’m Sergeant Candace Filmore of the Canadian Armed Services.”

“How did you know we were in a bag of shite?”

“One of our satellites picked up those two transports heading your way. We figured you might need a hand.”

32

The Earth recedes so fast that it is almost overwhelming as they watch through the ship’s front portal.

Within sixty seconds of having escaped the facility, L.I.N. deftly navigates the ship into orbit, with Kaetlyn and the others watching on, slack-jawed and amazed at the fluidity of the entire operation.

“My gawd,” says Shamus, breaking the taciturnity, “that was a blast from the past.”

L.I.N.’s image materializes. She smiles, “So, Captain, we are now a safe distance from any threat, at least for the moment.”

The three are still mesmerized and speechless as their eyes remain glued on the site of the Earth.

"Are you okay?" inquires L.I.N.

"Fine …" answers Kaetlyn. She forces her eyes to meet L.I.N.'s. "We've never been in space before, that's all…"

L.I.N. cuts her off. "Well, technically, you and Shamus have not been in space for nineteen years, twelve days and twenty-three hours, give or take a few minutes."

"And that feels like an eternity," adds Shamus.

"You all seem to be somewhat dehydrated; might I suggest that you divest yourselves of those bulky suits and imbibe one of our better drinks?"

"What about the virus?" asks Serena with a nervous tick in her voice.

"Ah, yes, the virus…" answers L.I.N. "I can assure you that the ship's atmosphere is hermetically sealed. Once you enter the antechamber, it automatically assesses the air for any contagion and purifies the system. The ship is free of any viral threat."

Tepidly, they divest themselves of the bulky suits, feeling a sense of freedom again.

"Are you sure we're safe out here?" asks Kaetlyn.

"My readings show 131 satellites in this geosynchronous region. None of them possess military weapons."

“Geosynchronous?” asks Serena.

“In reference to an orbital zone around a planet.”

“How can you be sure about the other satellites?” challenges Kaetlyn.

“I have scanned them for thermal and chemical constituents, and beyond the usual solar cells and batteries used to power them, I see no immediate threat. Of course, there are hundreds more satellites which are beyond my purview at this instant, so I will continue to scan new ones as they appear.”

“What about the Colonel and the others?” poses Shamus.

“I wouldn’t advise going back,” says L.I.N.

“We can’t just abandon them.”

L.I.N. nods. “I believe, if you asked Colonel Desmond, his response would be to focus on resolving the larger issue at hand.”

Kaetlyn sighs as she turns to Shamus and presses a hand to his arm. “She’s right. He did all of this so we could get away and use our resources to help stop the virus. If we go back, it could ruin everyone’s chances.”

Shamus’ jaw crimps tight.

“If the Captain agrees,” begins L.I.N. with a hitched brow at Kaetlyn, “I can dispatch a drone to inspect the area and provide us with on-going information as to the status of the Colonel and his team.”

"Please do that," answers Kaetlyn, "and stop calling me Captain."

33

Bikká and her brother exit the helicopter which was sent to pick them up, and are immediately ushered to a containment area at the Center for Disease Control (CDC) in Helsinki, where they are examined to verify that neither show signs of infection, and then, are led to a sterile room that has been prepared with a gurney and other equipment, and where a small team of people are standing by.

The Director himself introduces Bikká and then goes on to speak, "We've reviewed all the records and test samples you had at the Kemi facility, so, theoretically speaking, we should be able to match whatever is in your blood that saved you from the virus."

Bikká nods. "How bad is it?"

The Director shakes his head with a dour look. "There are already reports of cases in Oulu, only 500 kilometers to the north."

"My god," the words hush from her lips.

"At this rate of permeation, it will reach Helsinki in a matter of days. Our only redeeming feature right now, which might buy us more time, is that the prevailing winds have shifted northeasterly, but that is only to say that the Russians will get hit harder."

He turns to Bikká. "Are you ready to be poked and prodded?"

She nods as the others in the room take their stations.

34

Shamus sits staring out the front portal of the ship as they gently sweep around Earth at a speed that makes other satellites appear to be standing still.

He is not sure which feeling is more surreal; the fact that he was the engineer aboard this very ship a lifetime ago and seems to be remembering bits and pieces of it now, or that they just managed to escape a deadly altercation in Alaska.

He turns to Kaetlyn who is sitting silently staring out the portal. "You know …" he begins.

"What?"

"In all this time, since you've started remembering your … our past lives, I haven't heard you ask the obvious question?"

Kaetlyn tips her head at him. Her eyes are red and swollen from exhaustion, and her face is washed out from the exertion of their recent episode. “What question is that?”

“What was your name, you know, your identity back then – and for that matter, what did you even look like?”

Kaetlyn’s head bobs like a toy. “Doesn’t seem relevant to me?”

“Might help you remember more if you knew.”

Kaetlyn thinks on it before answering.” I thought of asking L.I.N. to fill in the blanks for me, but I am not ready yet to look at the face of my past life.” She sighs. “I’m still trying to cope with who I am right now and what’s happening with me, with us.”

“Yeah, I guess that makes sense.” He draws a deep breath and returns to staring out into space.

Kaetlyn continues to watch him, and in his face, she sees the repressed emotion, as if there is something, he is holding back from her. For all the details she has remembered over the past months since they started delving into her past life, the connection between Shamus and her, or more to the point, the love they once shared, had not yet breached the strongholds of whatever mental shielding kept her past life memories separate from the now. She liked Shamus. He was her closest friend now, next only to Serena, and of course, L.I.N., but… did she still love him in the same way that he still felt about her? She did not know.

He turns to her. "What?"

Her eyes drift for a moment, finding it hard to breach the subject. "I was thinking about what you said when we first met, the feeling that drove you to find me."

He grins. "Still haven't made peace with the fact that we were an item, uh?"

Again, she shrugs – a dismissive gesticulation that she uses more times than necessary. "It is more complicated than that. Remembering the details of how to fly this ship, how to launch the *Intervention*, countless details, are all coming back to me with increased clarity. And even though I remember us being together, the intimacy part of it …'"

"You mean how we felt about each other?"

"Yeah, it's not coming back the same way for me that you feel."

"You just need more time."

"I'm not trying to block it out, Shamus. I am willing for it to happen again, if it is meant to be, but … uhm …" she searches for the right words, "if you know anything about me by now, you know that I have never been the warm feely type. I was graced with intelligence, but my cup is half full when it comes to emotional sensitivity."

He shifts uncomfortably. "I don't buy that, Kaet. You might not be the feely-feely type, and you were not that way in our other life too, but your empathy is bigger than anyone I have ever known. You are putting your life on the line to save a world where countless people are threatening you every day. There isn't any greater empathy than that."

Kaetlyn is silent for a time.

He continues. "Look. I was compelled by a dream, by a feeling I shared with you years ago. I've never been naïve enough to believe that it would be the same for us this time round." He smiles, weakly as he sighs. "It doesn't hurt to dream it, right?"

She nods as she steals a look at Serena who is curled up on the third chair.

"Do you believe in karma?"

"Not really. Do you?"

"In a way, yeah, I do," answers Shamus.

"Why?"

"Karma is more about what we dream or what we secretly desire. Eventually, however far in the future, those dreams or desires catch up with us."

She watches him for a time before speaking. "Are you saying that our coming together again is fate, in the sense that you described?"

He nods. "Yeah, I do. Even though I did not fully understand it at the time, or why I was having those constant dreams about you, I knew, somehow, you had to exist because you were alive in my head, in my dreams." He pauses with a smile. "Maybe this is proof that love is trans-dimensional."

She tips her head at him. “Meaning?”

“Maybe love is the one thing that we all universally share that never really disappears no matter what happens to us, life after life?”

“Maybe...” she muses.

He slips from his chair and steps over to one corner of the control room and then points to a spot on the floor. “I have not remembered much about my past life on this ship, but I do remember some things. Do you know what happened here?” he points.

She shakes her head.

“This is where I cradled you in my arms until we died after the crash back then.”

Kaetlyn’s vision suddenly blurs as tears cloud her vision.

35

“They what?” exclaims President Tamp as he surges from his desk with a look of imminent rage pasted on his face like someone just tossed mud at him.

“The Canadian and Irish forces hit the Gordon Military Base in Alaska where we had the alien crafts.”

The President stands there, dumfounded by the news.

“How the hell could they do that?”

Madox P. Riley, Chairman of the Joint Chiefs of Staff, hands a paper to the President.

"We just received that memo from Vice-Admiral, Malcolm Calhoon, the Irish Joint Chief of Staff – my counterpart, in fact."

The President reads it and looks up. "Is this a joke? Who invades a US military base and then casually sends a memo about it!?"

"It's no joke, sir, we have eyes-on confirmation of the fact," the man's head wags.

"Arrogant pricks!" exclaims Tamp.

Willis tips his head at the man. "They're probably thinking the same thing."

President Tamp turns at him. "Is that supposed to be funny?"

"No, sir, I'm merely pointing out that for them to pull off such a brazen stunt, means they see it as reciprocity for what we've done."

Tamp flicks a dismissive hand to the air, "Who cares what they think. You were supposed to make this a neat operation. How on Earth did the Canadians and Irish get a whiff of the fact that we had the ships there?"

"We're not sure," answers Willis.

The President draws a breath and reads the memo again. "So … how the hell do we contain this mess?"

"The crafts are in orbit as we speak, sir."

"And?"

"Well, as that memo states, the Irish plan to use the alien technology to help stem the advance of the virus on Severny Island."

"Yeah, I read that much, Admiral – get to the point?"

"Sir," continues Willis, "my point is that while we missed a window of opportunity, we are still holding the ace card. Everyone knows that we have proprietary claim on that craft based on the 1973 Space Acco…"

The President raises a hand. "Let me cut you off there, Willis. That is being naïve if you think for a second that accord has any real value right now. I would say this," he waves the paper in the air, "is evidence that they do not give a shit about the Accord of '73."

The Chairman of the Joint Chiefs of Staff, speaks. "Mr. President, before coming here with this news, I met with the other Chiefs, and it is our view that we must take any measures necessary to get that craft back into our possession."

Tamp's face reddens with restrained anger. "Oh really!? They know we stole those crafts. They've got us in an awkward position, so how do you propose to do that?"

Madox continues. "First of all, it is a stand-off. We took the crafts, and they invaded our base and stole them back. Quid pro quo. At this stage no one's going to expose the other."

Tamp exhales to calm his temper. "Okay, what's your new proposal?"

"We propose two contingencies." He nods at Admiral Willis who takes it from there.

Willis steps up to the plate. "The first approach, obviously, will be to simply demand that they turn the craft over to us as soon as they have completed this plan to cap-off the fissures in the Severny region. The Irish will concede eventually, because they know they must, but I am not so sure about this young lady, Kaetlyn O'Sullivan, who has a mind of her own in this regard. So, failing that, we go with plan two."

"Which is?"

"ADX has two covert satellites in orbit, which we financed of course, each armed with the ADX-SR missiles. These missiles deliver a powerful electro-magnetic pulse…"

President Tamp cuts him off with an imperious flick of his hand. "I know the technical details, Willis … so that's your best plan, use this EMP again?"

"Sir, we know that once they finish the job on Severny, they plan to go back to the Russian air base nearby. That is when we will force the ship's computer to engage the same tactics it does every time there is a threat to it."

"Like you did on the Irish coast?"

"Yes. We'll make sure that we pick a time when there are no passengers inside the craft and spook it again, with another EMP blast over that base."

"That's no guarantee that it will return to orbit?"

"No, it is not, but we're counting on the fact that this computer, L.I.N. will do the logical thing this time and go into orbit to avoid any further complications. Once it is there, we'll launch the SRs from the ADX satellite."

"You're gambling, Admiral."

"Yes, it is a toss of the dice, but we believe it is a fairly justifiable approach."

"And if it doesn't go into orbit?"

"Then we'll be ready to launch another SR and take it down."

The President's head wags. "This is a weak approach."

Madox waltzes back into the dialogue. "Mr. President, we have to keep in mind that the only thing that can force that craft to evacuate an area, that we know of, is an EMP, and the only thing that can incapacitate it, and hopefully the drone ship attending it, is a good dose of EMP. We have the most effective means of delivering that kind of power – no one else has anything as intelligent or effective as the SR series of missiles. It isn't a question of knocking it out of the sky, it is a question of doing it at the right time so that we are there first to scoop it up."

Willis adds, "Mr. President, it's all about the optics at this point, and anything we do or say will be questionably perceived by the competition. But I assure you that if the Russians showed up, or the Chinese, or North Korea, and they retrieved those crafts, the world would have a bigger meltdown about the matter than if America plucked them from the sea."

The President paces the room for a time. Two thoughts are storming through his head. The upcoming elections and his shot at a second term in office; and the financial pot of gold that the alien technology will bring once they repurpose it.

He finally stops pacing and turns to them.

"Do it, but don't mess it up this time, Willis, because if you do, I will throw you under the bus myself.

36

"Colonel, how bad is it at your end," asks Kaetlyn who sits in front of the console of the ship, looking at him through a holographic screen which L.I.N. provides at the snap of … well, it is not really fingers, more like digital coding.

He sighs. "You want the sugar-coated version or the truth?" he begins, trying to lighten the moment.

"I could have L.I.N. hack the systems and tell me, but I'd prefer hearing it from you."

"We've managed to evacuate around 70% of the population in Belfast, pushing them to a staging area in the south where ships from the mainland are piling in to help ferry them to the Continent. We haven't even started to address the dead."

"Oh god, I don't even want to think about the death toll."

"Don't bother, lass. Just be ready to start the process on Severny when they call you in."

"Who is our contact?"

"The Russian military is overseeing and coordinating the entire operation, so you will be hearing from a Colonel, Karina Osipova. She'll be your contact throughout the process so that you don't have to interface with anyone else in Russia."

"May I ask," intercedes L.I.N., "where they stand currently?"

"They're currently using aerial drones with spectrometers that measure composition and density, and I'm told they've isolated twenty-one main fissures, the most concentrated leakage points from the icecap. Engineers and drillers are now arriving on Severny, and they'll prepare those locations for the next steps, the last of which, involves you."

"By preparing you mean they will fill the fissures with slag – correct?" says L.I.N.

"You seem to be updated, yes. Once they fill up the holes with the slag, you'll fly in and do your magic."

L.I.N. smiles. "Far from magic, Colonel. In your language, it translates to TAP or **T**ransmutation-**A**lteration-**P**rocess – a technology that permutates, as in rearranging, the molecular structure of matter from one state to another," she answers.

He shakes his head. "It's still looks like magic to me," he grins.

"When we've done it, what are they estimating this will do in terms of slowing the virus?" asks Kaetlyn.

Desmond answers, "The optimistic view, 40% reduction."

"But the virus will still be leaking out from other areas on the icecap, right?" enters Shamus.

"Yes, but at a weaker intensity." His face sobers. "The truth is that this operation will be like putting a band aid on a bleeding artery. So long as the icecap keeps melting, the virus will eventually escape. We are just buying time for ourselves – that's all."

37

After the call, Shamus stretches out in his chair and is soon in a deep sleep.

Only Kaetlyn remains awake, even though the chains of fatigue weigh heavily on her.

With her eyes fixed on the forward portal, she watches as the tip of North Africa peeks through a cloud cover obscuring the Mediterranean.

"A penny for your thoughts," says L.I.N. as her image appears nearby. "That is what people in your world say, correct?"

Kaetlyn shakes herself from her reverie. "I guess."

"You seem morose."

"Morose would be an upgrade right now."

"That's understandable."

"Hmm," Kaetlyn utters. "You're beginning to sound like Serena."

"I wish I could empathize more, but my circuitry simply does not allow me to synthesize emotion. I was designed to maximize the potential of logic and intelligence, Kaetlyn."

"I meant no insult. I just wish I could remain as objective as you are about all of this."

"I'll take that as a compliment," says L.I.N. as her holographic image shifts to the middle of the room, and for the first time in all their encounters, she stands there as a fully formed figure, revealing the stature and beauty of the race she represents. Silver braids of hair adorn her head and fall to the small of her back. A tall beauty, with an elongated torso, slim features, and those eyes, as green as emeralds.

"In all this time," begins L.I.N. with a look of curiosity, "you have not asked me more than a few questions about your home world? Why is that?"

Kaetlyn draws a deep breath and exhales. "It's kind of complicated, don't you think?"

"It is only complicated because you refuse to accept the fact that you are not from this place."

Kaetlyn turns to her. "I was born here, so, it sort of makes it my home, too."

"You have lived nineteen years on this planet, a mere blip in the spectrum of time."

Kaetlyn throws an angry hand to the air. "God, L.I.N., why are you choosing now to talk about this when my world, that world," she points to the planet, "is in a shite storm?"

L.I.N. approaches and stops in front of Kaetlyn. "Because it is relevant to the circumstances that must be faced."

"How is it relevant?"

"You have only accepted a tiny portion of the truth about who you are. Your refusal to open all the doors to your past is shackling you, Kaetlyn. You are holding yourself back, and to that degree, you are making the accomplishment of this mission not only more difficult, but potentially, impossible."

Kaetlyn kicks off the chair and lands next to L.I.N. "So, now you're putting this on me?"

"I am not accusing you of anything except a failure to accept full responsibility."

Kaetlyn suppresses her anger. "Okay, let's assume you're right, and I open up all the doors' to my past - what does that accomplish? I mean," she waves an angry hand around the ship, "what have we accomplished so far! Nothing, not a thing!"

L.I.N. walks to the other end of the control room and speaks as she looks through a portal at the Earth. "First of all, that statement is not true, and you know it. The fact that this ship was exhumed precisely while your past life revealed itself to you, has caught the attention of the world and it has started a ripple-effect that is and will lead to changes throughout the culture."

"More like a shite-storm if you ask me. I don't see a lot of effort to stop global warming."

L.I.N. points a finger at her. "This is my point, Kaetlyn. You are failing to see the bigger picture because you are still embroiled in something else."

"What!?"

L.I.N.'s demeanor remains resolute. "I sense that you are holding onto guilt for having failed your mission, and the fact that you refuse to let go of that and accept that the mission is not done, is preventing you from taking charge again.'

Kaetlyn slumps into a morose state as she leans against the chair. "I did fail. Ice caps are melting, a deadly virus is killing everything in its path …"

L.I.N. cuts her off, "And all of that would have happened anyhow. You made a tactical error, Kaetlyn, when you misestimated the state of their defense systems. I also made the same error, I failed to assess the state of their orbital satellites fast enough. So, I too am responsible for what happened." She steps closer, her brilliantly green eyes fixed on Kaetlyn's. "But that is the past, and the present demands that we finish what we started."

Kaetlyn huffs. "As if I could do a better job than you – the most advanced Ai … blah blah blah."

"Now, you are just lashing out. Indeed, I am smart, but my ability to think and act is limited by the parameters of my programming protocols. There is a limit to what I can do, Kaetlyn, but there is no limit to what you can do."

Kaetlyn is silent as she digests her words. "What do you mean?"

L.I.N. points to the planet. "I am a machine – a synthetic intelligence. You, however, and every person down there, are something entirely different, you are the product of something extraordinary. If you could see the timeline of the cosmos as I see it through the immense knowledge stored in my data base, you would see just how amazing sentient life is, how amazing every person down there is. I did not intend this to be a lesson on theology or the philosophical aspects of existentiality," says L.I.N. with almost professorial-like cadence in her voice, "but the fact remains, that the game on Earth has become, to a very large degree, about survival inside a very tiny bubble – and if they truly understood who they really are, and what happens to them in the so called “afterlife”, that there exists no god or gods anywhere in the known Universe except for themselves, that nothing is going to save them except themselves, that culture would undergo massive transformation as a matter of course, and for the better.”

“Your point?”

“Maybe…” she pauses,” the timing is better now than ever. We would have been more effective twenty years ago, but, given the circumstances at that time, it would not have worked or been permanent. But now, your presence here is a matter of global interest. Everyone is watching you, Kaetlyn – and therein lies the sincere hope – and you could give it to them if you decided to.”

38

Standing within the room, what is colloquially referred to as *The Bubble* at the CDC because of its shape and its walls of glass, with a team of scientists and virologists, Bikká waits as the Director of the Finnish Center for Disease Control moves to the front of the group.

“The blood samples taken from Bikká some hours ago,” he begins with a nod her way, “have thankfully revealed traces of an antiviral compound, which, when applied to this, now officially labelled the Severnus virus, or SV, neutralized it.”

The room lightens noticeably, as people receive the news with great relief.

“We don’t have much to work with at this point, and moreover, the research notes from the Kemi facility showed that particular antiviral cocktail underwent an incubation period of 23 days before it matured and could be used.”

That comment drops a cloud over the group, like a heavy blanket falling from the sky.

“Obviously,” he continues, “considering our circumstances, 23 days is entirely out of the question – as by that time, Severnus will have eviscerated most of our population. So… you are the best minds in all of Finland when it comes to virology, put your heads together, and figure out how we can solve this.”

The room suddenly erupts into a cacophony of dialogues.

A figure steps up to Bikká, touches her arm and motions her aside from the group. “May we speak in private?” asks the man in well-spoken English, with a hint of Russian. “It really is a matter of quite some urgency.”

Bikká follows him to the canteen where he promptly leads her to a corner table away from others.

My name is Yuri Lebedev – like you, I am a virologist, however, today I am acting as ambassador from the Moscow Ministry of Health."

"Okay," her eyebrows narrow with a questioning aspect, "What can I do for you, Yuri."

"Are you familiar with the history of Severny Island?"

"Not really."

"There is an important backstory which you should know."

"How is this relevant to the crisis?"

"Please bear with me."

She nods as she sips her coffee.

"In 1961, my government exploded the *Tzar Bomba*, the most powerful nuclear warhead ever detonated on Earth."

"I have heard of it. We Finns were keeping an eye on you during the Cold War era – remember?"

"Yes, of course you were," he lets off a diplomatic chuckle to lighten the moment. "The *Tzar Bomba*, was 1500 times more powerful than the bombs dropped on Japan during WW II. So powerful in fact, that at ground zero, it carved out a massive crater in the Severny icecap, having melted away layers of ice that had been there for quite possibly, millions of years," he paused. "As a consequence, it unleashed a pathogen which had been buried in the ice for who knows how long."

Bikká raises a brow.

"How the pathogen got there, whether it was a remnant of the Ice Age, or whether it was carried on the back of a meteorite that crashed into Severny, no one knew at the time."

Bikká feels her skin begin to crawl. "How did they find out about the virus?"

"After the *Tzar* was ignited, a military detail and a handful of scientists remained near the blast site to study its effects. Just days after the blast, every person at that camp was found dead. The military poured in and began to study the carnage and soon found out about the pathogen."

"Are we talking about the same virus, Yuri?"

He nods. "Yes. Same virus, same symptoms, same lethality."

Shock spreads across her face like a strong wind. "You guys knew it was there in the early 1960s?"

"We did. Fortunately, the *Tzar* explosion only released a small amount of the virus, unlike today, which is titanic in comparison."

Bikká is still grappling with the shock.

Yuri continues, "The good news is that they also developed an antidote."

A wave of emotion ripples across her face, betraying the mix of joy, confusion and anger suddenly bursting inside. "Let me get this straight, you guys knew about the virus sixty years ago, and you had an antivirus, and this is just coming up now?"

“I understand how this looks, but please, before you react, hear me out.”

She crimps her jaw and nods.

“The early 1960s was the height of the Cold War. I lived through it. You, however, only studied about it since you are so young. Russia and America were building up the means of annihilating one another. It was a crazy time for all of us, and unfortunately, those in power in Russia saw the virus as a tool, something that could be weaponized.”

“Are you serious?”

He shrugs. “Unfortunately, that is the nature of war, Bikká. They went on to build an underground base in the southern part of Severny, where the virus was harvested from the icecap, and then stored in cannisters for deployment. They also developed the vaccine.”

“So, they couldn’t weaponize it without a way of controlling it.”

He shakes his head. “No. They had to have a way to protect Russian military. It is not as if the virus distinguishes between Russian or American. It kills indiscriminately, as we now know.”

“How much vaccine are we talking about, Yuri?”

“Assuming none of the cannisters have been compromised after sitting there for nearly sixty years, roughly 50 of them – enough to vaccinate about a million troops at the time, if needed.”

Bikká struggles with the storm of emotions inside. "Why are you telling me this? Why isn't your government talking to mine about this?"

"At first, we did not know if it was the same virus. When the outbreak started at Severny this past week, it triggered alarms in our system and we sent teams of scientists up there, and after significant assessment, they confirmed it was the same pathogen. We are, as if this moment, assessing the vaccine that was developed back in the early sixties on an isolated group to determine its efficacy."

"And?"

"So far, the results are positive."

"I'm confused, why are we sitting here discussing this in secrecy, when millions of people are in its cross hairs, my nation included?"

He leans in. "The problem, as you may well surmise, is a delicate one – which is why I am here speaking to you and which is why my government is not talking to yours, or anyone, about this matter."

Bikká leans back in her chair, studying him for a moment, and then it strikes her, like a light suddenly turning on in a dark room. "Oh, I get it, you don't want the world to know that you guys knew the virus was there sixty years ago, buried in that icecap, and now, you don't want them to know that there were plans to weaponize it."

"You understand the delicacy of the matter." He pauses, "Consider our position, Bikká. The West is very quick to demonize Russia. Given any opportunity, we are profiled as the bad guys, and frankly, my government is not interested in being character assassinated over this matter. This is not something we are proud of, it is a stigma for us, a ghost from our past. That is why I was sent here to negotiate the matter."

"Negotiate what?"

"We will provide the research notes, the formula, and sufficient cannisters of the vaccine to assist you in developing more, on one condition …"

"What condition?"

"Complete discretion. No one can ever know of this backstory I have told you. No one."

"But … once you start vaccinating people with the existing stuff, isn't word going to leak?"

He smiles. "Leave that to us." We Russians are good at keeping secrets."

"Okay, so what do you want of me?"

"You are Finland's top virologist. I trust you as a fellow scientist, not as a politician or otherwise, to take our proposal to your CDC Director and implore him to agree that if we release the vaccine to you, that the backstory will never be divulged - ever."

Bikká is momentarily silent.

Yuri continues, "He will need to work out a narrative that explains how this formula was suddenly derived, but that should be simple considering that you have already opened the door – given that you survived the virus, and they now know why. So, the fact that the Finnish virologists produce the antivirus, will not raise any questioning brows from the rest of the world." He pauses. "Beyond that, there can never be any mention of the truth." He leans back and waits a moment for her to digest it all. "If, however, he cannot agree to these terms, then this conversation never happened."

"That's rather brutal."

"That would be entirely your choice, not mine," he answers.

"How can this be so complicated?"

"It is quite simple, Bikká. You and I see the world differently. As scientists, we see it in terms of black and white, fact, not fiction. However, those in government positions do not perceive it the same way. They worry about the optics and the countless shades in between, and believe me, there will be those in power in other places, who would happily use this information to criminalize my nation or worse."

She thinks about it for a moment, but something still hangs with her. "Why us, why Finland?"

Yuri tips his head at her. "For obvious reasons, your blood has just provided a window for the vaccine that can save the world; and, if I am not mistaken, Finland is currently facing Armageddon in less than what…?"

She draws a breath. "Days – a week at most," the words hush from her lips with dread.

"Exactly. If that virus continues its current rate of permeation, Finland is facing the ultimate apocalypse before most any nation."

"But why not America, why not use this as leverage to finally bury the hatchet and make peace? This could be the very thing that stops the animosity between you and them?"

He grins. "Your age makes you naïve to the dynamics that have fueled the prolonged animosity between our two nations. It is much more than just Communism, which has been dead in our nation since 1989. Logically, that hatchet should have been buried long ago, but there is something that continues to fuel the hate, the suspicions and the insistence on profiling us as the enemy to the American way of life."

"What?"

"American fundamentalism. It forms the thread of their mentality, particularly those who run that nation, and as such, they require a devil, a demon, to blame things on, something evil that threatens their way of life and which justifies creating and maintaining a massive military establishment that can be used to forward that fundamentalism. For decades, it was the threat of Communism and the Cold War. Today it is terrorism. Tomorrow – who knows? That fundamentalism is ingrained in their way of seeing the world, and Americans are made to perceive good and bad based on those fundamentalist views. It is a veil that obscures truth, and because America is such a large nation, a world of its own, Americans tend to be insulated from the rest of the world. For that reason, it is easy to use official proclamations and media to create whatever mindset they want, such as profiling Islam as the training camp of terrorism, or Russia as a demonic force intent on destroying the American way of life. And yet, laughably, American fundamentalism is its own brand of extremism, and one which empowers their dogma. They believe, implicitly, that they are the best and most powerful nation on the planet, and that their brand of democracy justifies invading other nations and forcing themselves upon them. It is quite insulting, to the say the least, to the rest of the world. Go ask the people of Iraq or Afghanistan how they feel about having been invaded and infused with American "democracy" and you will find quite a different picture than that presented by the American information machinery." He pauses to sip his coffee. "Believe me, we considered having a dialogue with them about the virus and offering the vaccine to them, but to do so would require macheting our way through veils of distrust, decades of objectification and false perceptions of who we are, and frankly, we didn't have time for it, and neither do you, and that is why I am here talking to you about this matter."

"You make them sound like the bad guys."

He shrugs. “I am merely answering your question and pressing the point that perception is more powerful than the truth.”

She draws a breath and exhales.

“What now?”

He tips his head at her. “The ball is in your court, Bikká. What do you want to do?”

39

Rockwell Sims sits facing the large screen in the comfort of his luxurious office atop the ADX building in Palo Alto, California, courtesy of the American taxpayers, while watching and listening as the Admiral of the US Air Force speaks.

Willis’ face is carved with deep lines, trenched out by worry and stress, and his skin, paler than usual, manifests the pressure he is enduring.

“I just come out of a meeting with the Joint Chiefs of Staff.”

“And?”

“We need to make this right, Sims. We need both of those crafts in our hands with no more screw ups.”

Sims tips his head at the screen. “If you’re inferring that we fucked up the operation in Alaska, I’d like to point out that the Canadians picked up on your military transports on *their* side of the border, and that's where that train derailed."

Willis tempers his approach. "Granted, those were unforeseen circumstances. The point being that we must get it right this time. We need those crafts, Rockwell. YOU need them. The stuff in that ship, in the mind of that computer, it will break every paradigm and put us so far ahead of the tech-curve that no one will ever catch up with us."

"I know that," he answers with distemper. "Anyhow, I've had my techies review the plan and it should work, providing you guys get there fast enough to scoop them up before anyone else does."

"I'm coordinating all our resources," answers Willis, "we'll be ready once you knock them out of orbit."

When the call ends, Rockwell sits silently staring out the window.

His usual bravado has been weakened somehow – a crack in his armor had appeared, and he feels vulnerable for the first time in an exceedingly long while.

A vagrant thought passes through his mind, *it is time to walk away from all of this before it goes completely sideways,* but then another compelling voice reminds him that he is contractually committed to his one and only client – the U.S. military, so walking away simply is not an option.

40

"What's the latest in Severny?" asks Kaetlyn.

L.I.N.'s face materializes in front of her. "My findings corroborate what their scientists have found. There are twenty-one main fissures or cracks in the icecap where the emission of the virus is strongest. However, there are more, smaller ones, which will have to be addressed as well. You might also be interested to know that there appears to be a foreign object lodged deep with that icepack."

"Really? A meteorite or what?"

"I would have to analyze it further to determine its exact nature."

Kaetlyn sighs as she pauses mid-stride. "I'm worried, L.I.N."

"About?"

"How effective do you think this handling will be?"

"It is difficult to say, but I would estimate at the very least, a 27% reduction in permeation of Severnus once the fissures are sealed."

"Which means that we still have to move fast on dealing with the real issue."

"Global warming, yes," answers L.I.N. "Assuming we have the cooperation needed to achieve Net-Zero-Emissions."

Kaetlyn is silent for a time, before switching the topic of discussion from the moroseness of the virus to something more interesting. “I’m curious, why you haven’t mentioned anything about reporting back to your home world?”

“It’s your home world too,” responds L.I.N. with a grin and a hiked brow. “And what makes you think I have not been performing my due diligence?”

“An assumption, I guess, but then again, you haven’t mentioned anything about it.”

“It’s part of my primary protocols to provide on-going information about the status of our mission. I assumed you knew.”

“You are still calling it “our mission.”

“Because it is – we are, however delayed in our time frame, pursuing the primary agenda.”

“Has there been any response from them?”

“Not yet.”

“What do you think that means?”

“It is difficult to say. The circumstances of having a ship resurface after nineteen years and resume, however indirectly, its mission, is as confusing to them as it has been to us.”

Kaetlyn leans back in her chair. “Tell me about your … I mean, our world?”

“How much do you remember?”

“Vague bits, just dim memories when I was in the coma after the shooting.”

L.I.N. brings up a new holographic image. "This is where you came from" she tips her head at the image of a planet, possessing multiple rings girding it, like Saturn."

Kaetlyn's eyes are transfixed on the blue orb girded by silvery bands, hanging in the blackness of space.

"What is it called?"

"Azoria."

"How far away is it?

"Many light years."

Kaetlyn turns to her. "Are you saying that this ship can travel faster than the speed of light?"

"You still have much to relearn, Kaetlyn. Azoria, and most of the other planets in the Federation, have long since perfected space travel using TSC."

"TSC?"

"*Trans-Spatial-Closure*. The immense distances between solar systems and galaxies would be prohibitive to contact with other civilizations, were it not for TSC. With it, we have learned to navigate the stars using the cosmic threads."

"Like worm holes?"

L.I.N. nods. "Yes, the concept is similar; they are anomalous energy vortexes which run throughout the galaxy. Our ship is equipped with a quantum drive that can travel well beyond the speed of light, but even so, distances are so vast that it would take years to go to and from other solar systems. TSC reduces travel time to a fraction – literally, making our original trip here to Earth just a matter of weeks."

"My god, that's incredible."

"It is," smiles L.I.N. "Imagine …" she pauses.

"What?"

"Imagine if humanity could just stop fighting with one another, learn to respect and tolerate their differences, live peacefully, and devote all their potential to reaching the stars? The unlimited grandness of the Universe would suddenly open up to them." L.I.N. shakes her head, as if frustrated. "Based on celestial studies, there are enough planets and suns out there, Kaetlyn, for every one of the nine billion people here on Earth to own one or even several of them, without greed, without war, without fighting or killing one another over a small piece of rock."

Silence ensues as Kaetlyn continues to stare at the planet.

L.I.N. tips her head questioningly. "What are your intentions, Kaetlyn? Now that you know who you are, do you plan to return to Azoria when we have finished what we came to do, or will you remain here?"

Kaetlyn chuckles. "That's a funny question."

"Why is it funny?"

She looks up to L.I.N. with an impish grin. "I've been out of the game for nineteen years, L.I.N., so I assume my contract with my former employer ended back then when I died."

"There are different schools of thought on that matter."

Kaetlyn's head wags back and forth – feeling her disputatious troops lining up for the impending argument. "I feel a lecture coming my way."

"If I must, I'd like to remind you that you are, for all intents and purposes, and to use a rather poor term, an immortal being – like everyone else down there."

L.I.N. moves closer, situating herself in front of Kaetlyn. "I admire you, Kaetlyn. In fact, if there is an emotional spark anywhere within my neural matrix, it would be envy."

Kaetlyn's face screws up. "Envy? Why?"

"You are alive, and moreover, you're aware of being aware not only as Kaetlyn, but as the person you once were – you're not limited by the memories of one life. I, on the other hand, have finite borders, digital markers which define my existence. That makes you so much more than I can ever be."

"Don't undersell yourself."

"I appreciate the laud, but I know my limitations. I know that I can be unplugged. I can be hit with an EMP blast hard enough to fry my very circuitry. I know that once I go offline, I may never again return. And yet," she seems almost sad in aspect, "over these past months, experiencing everything as we have, and being shut down into an oblivious state of unconsciousness two times, I started to appreciate how wonderful it must feel to be truly alive – like you and all the others."

Kaetlyn feels an odd trembling inside as warm tears pool and streak her cheeks.

"Have I upset you?" asks L.I.N.

"No, in fact, you just made me feel better about myself."

"Why?" probes L.I.N.

Kaetlyn wipes her eyes. "I've have always felt different…like I stepped off the train at the wrong station. I have struggled with that feeling my whole life, but now … as I get a grip on who I am, that sense of disenfranchisement is ebbing." She pauses to reflect as her eyes sink to the floor. "I just wish others could reconcile my differences without feeling threatened."

"You mean all the threats to your life?" responds L.I.N.

"It's just so weird to be in this position. I just don't understand people, how they could perceive my existence as a threat to theirs – it's completely incomprehensible to me."

L.I.N. smiles. "I'd like to offer some perspective, if I may."

She waves a hand, "Go ahead."

"I have at my fingertips the knowledge of thousands of civilizations, gathered and stored in my matrix, information accumulated over countless eons by the people who built me, your people, Kaetlyn; and it struck me as I recently reviewed many of those civilizations, looking for comparative data to better understand Earth's situation, that there was a commonality between most of the early contact with them – do you know what that factor is?"

Kaetlyn shakes her head.

"First or early contact with new cultures or new civilizations, wherever they were located, almost inevitably was met with fear."

"That's understandable, people fear what they don't know."

"Yes, they do, but am referring to a visceral fear, one that is entirely illogical for any sentient being."

"How so?"

"Take my perspective as an A.I. Imagine if my matrix was designed so that I reacted viscerally, first with fear and distrust, not logic – how accurate and useful would my existence and conclusions be in terms of your survival?"

"Pretty poor," answers Kaetlyn.

"Yes. And on the other end of this spectrum, it was observable that when a civilization, a people, collectively speaking, stepped over the threshold and started using their innate ability to think and understand as its platform, instead of reacting with fear and violence, that was the demarcation point from which that civilization or group, large or small, moved from a state of primitive brutality, to an advanced one."

"Well, we're certainly not there yet, here on Earth?"

L.I.N. grins. "Clearly not. You are different in their eyes, not only because you claim to have come from another world, but because you have shaken the platform, the very stanchions of their world. Your existence defies all their paradigms – and that threatens them."

L.I.N. tips her head at the holo which morphs, showing clusters of stars, with accentuated glowing dots interspersed. "That is a picture, an actual image, of what you call the Milky Way – just a small piece of the entire Universe. Each glowing dot you see is a solar system with documented civilized worlds, and if I magnify the image …" the holo suddenly morphs in size, "you can see just how small the Milky Way is in comparison to a mere mockup of the size and extent of the Universe as a whole, but no one knows for sure, not yet." She smiles. "You see, even our civilization has barely scratched the surface. It defies all the paradigms being taught here on Earth, where people are struggling to accept the concept of alien life forms, and in many cases, are simply in denial about it and want to believe that humans are alone in this Universe – a concept that is not only delusional, but simply arrogant."

Kaetlyn is mesmerized by the image.

"You see, Kaet," she grins, "there are many places out there, within reach of Earth – if only humanity would stop fighting amongst themselves and focus on achieving their true potentiality."

Kaetlyn turns to L.I.N. "I assume we were not the first to visit Earth back then?"

L.I.N. nods. "Far from it. There are loads of documented visitations to this planet. I believe that those who came before us, and even after our fateful crash, were interested to see how the culture was progressing. Decidedly, they were not interested in presenting themselves."

Kaetlyn's head bobs. "No one wants to be friends with a planet of people who fight and kill one another over stupid shite, is that it?"

"In so many words, yes."

"And yet…" she pauses, "the people who sent us here, they still saw fit to try and save Earth."

"Of course. Humanity deserves a chance to get out there in the stars, and even in my humble estimation, they have shown the ability to change and advance."

Kaetlyn draws a deep breath and exhales. "So, all we have to do is make sure they have that chance."

41

Sitting in the comfort of their living room, Harry and Claire O'Sullivan watch the Telly to take their minds off the crisis.

It is a surreal scene, considering that the media, and most stations that remain on the air, are broadcasting nothing but the crisis and the fact that Ireland itself has been reduced to a ghost town and graveyard.

They know what is headed their way, sitting on the remote southwesterly coast of Ireland, and unlike most of the folks in the small town of Bantry who have already abandoned the area, Harry remains obstinate to the last moment, even as a special military convoy, courtesy of Colonel Desmond himself, is on the way to pick them up and evacuate them to a waiting ship off the coast.

They watch, over a cup of hot tea, as the BBC special report shows masses of people offering a collective prayer for humanity.

Earlier in the day, the World Health Organization released an update on SEVERNUS, and the coordinated plan to try and stop it, or at least, inhibit its outpouring from the source.

What the world knows is that two alien crafts, commanded by a nineteen-year-old Irish woman, already the center of the storm, are headed for Severny Island to help close the leaking dam.

Tiring of the dreaded news, Harry steps to the old oak cabinet and breaks-out his best bottle of Tullamore Dew Irish Whiskey. He unscrews the cap with a lover's touch and tips the bottle over his teacup and pours in a generous amount.

"I'm scared, Harry," says Claire with dread in her voice.

"We'll be fine."

She shakes her head. "It is Kate I'm worried about, and Shamus and Serena too. They're flying into the eye of the storm up there." She turns to him. "What if they get attacked again? What if the Yanks or the Russians, or someone else decides to shoot 'em down?"

Harry steps over to her and tips the bottle of Tullamore into the cup she holds.

"Kaet knows what she is doing. Now …" he eyes the cup in her hand, bottoms up!" he commands just as the military vehicles arrive in front of their home.

42

Standing on the open tarmac, Kaetlyn feels the hand of an angry wind pounding into her hazmat suit.

She looks up and down the entire length of the runway, where Russian fighter jets are lined up like soldiers in perfect formation. Their pilots sit in a nearby building, ready in an instant to be called into action if anything should happen, while Russian military personnel, armed to the teeth, form a ring around the area where the two alien crafts have landed.

Kaetlyn can't help but feel a sense of irony as she sizes up the forces amassed by the Russians to protect her and the ships, considering that several months earlier, they had tried to steal one of the crafts and secret it to a Russian base, but were foiled at the last minute, and thankfully so, because the confrontation between them and the Yanks did not portend well.

It had been seven hours since they landed at Vorkuta, a coal-mining city on the Russian Arctic rim, and staging area for what everyone was calling ***Operation Top Up***.

The locale had been chosen as the HQ for the operation since the center of the storm was on Russian ground. Moreover, and more to the point, Vorkuta, besides being a strategic military base, also had a large mining facility nearby, which had accumulated a literal mountain of slag, the stony waste matter separated from metals during the smelting or refining of ore, which was now being loaded onto a train of trucks and would be used to plug up the holes in the ice cap on Severny.

It was the fastest and most readily available source of material, in sufficient quantity, they hoped, to fill the fissures in the ice cap, after which, the alien craft would perform its part.

Their contact, Colonel, Karina Osipova, approaches.

Karina, a Russian military attaché who speaks perfect English, has been their contact and host, providing not only food and drinks, but continuous updates on the progress of the operation.

She stops in front of them, with a friendly, yet militarily controlled smile on her lips.

"I have just confirmed that the last of the trucks are loaded with the slag and are on their way to Severny. Meanwhile, several trucks have already arrived at the first two coordinates."

"How many trucks in total?" asks Shamus.

"223," she answers.

"That's a lot of slag," he comments.

"Based on estimations, it is hoped this will suffice, but we are prepared to send more trucks if needed." She peers through her mask at Kaetlyn. "To recap, given time for the slag to arrive and be unloaded in the fissures, will take approximately sixty hours.

During this time, you will coordinate with the lead engineer at each location, who will cue you as to when you may begin your process."

"TAP," offers Kaetlyn with a smile.

"Yes. Fascinating process just to think of it," responds Karina. "Is there anything else you require?" she asks.

Kaetlyn shakes her head. "No. I think L.I.N. has everything she needs."

Karina nods her head. "I would like to meet this L.I.N. someday."

"Maybe we can arrange a tour," answers Kaetlyn with a smile.

They say their goodbyes and enter the warm embrace of the ship. Divesting themselves of the hazmat suits in the antechamber, they enter the control room where they find L.I.N. waiting.

"We are ready," she announces.

Kaetlyn hops up on the chair. "How long before we arrive to the first location?"

"90 seconds – give or take a few," answers L.I.N. without delay.

"Wow," exclaims Shamus. "That's hardly even a trip."

"If you prefer a more scenic route, I can take us on an orbital loop around the planet," responds L.I.N. with a playful grin.

"We'll skip the scenic version, thanks. Cast off, Mr. Sulu," says Kaetlyn.

L.I.N. cocks her head to one side with a quizzical aspect. "I am not familiar with that term."

Kaetlyn waves her off. "You're obviously not a Trekkie. Just go!"

43

There are moments in modern history when the world was brought to pause, gripped by circumstances that affected all humanity.

When Neil Armstrong placed his foot on the moon in 1969, it changed the world, proving that man could reach beyond our planet.

When the Iron Curtain crumbled in 1989, it ended the Cold War and announced the unilateral failure of Communism.

And now, as two alien crafts head toward a region of the Russian Arctic, about to do something that no one has ever witnessed before – millions upon millions are glued to their smart phones, tablets, and televisions.

"We have arrived at the first coordinates," announces L.I.N. as she brings the ship round for them to see the activity below. The scene on the view screen shows teams of workers, trudging through the snow in their bulky hazmat suits as people and equipment are moved beyond the perimeter of the first fissure which is now topped up with a small mountain of slag.

They wait in anticipation for the signal announcing that they can proceed.

It takes only moments before the façade of white that dominates the domain, is violated by the intense red flare flaming up into the sky.

"Let 'er rip, L.I.N." says Kaetlyn.

L.I.N. deftly lowers the ship to within an arm's length of a narrow shaft drilled into the icecap, now filled with slag.

Dozens of workers, engineers, military personnel and scientists, stand-off at a distance, filming the entire process, while Russian television crews broadcast it live to the rest of the world.

After so much preparation, hours of drilling and then filling the hole with slag, they watch as the anticlimactic moment passes in just a matter of seconds.

No one really understands the process which L.I.N. calls TAP, or how it works or what to expect. There is no flash of energy. No sound. No visible anything for that matter.

But to those watching, what they do see is solid heap of slag suddenly transmutes into another form, all in the space of a second or two.

Shamus is stunned by what he sees. "It didn't melt or boil," he says.

"It doesn't work like that," begins L.I.N. "TAP is a permutation technique which simply reconfigures the molecular structure of matter from one form to another." She flashes up a hologram so they can see more closely. "If you touched that slag now, it would feel cold."

"But is it a liquid or what?"

"No, you are looking at solid matter. As I said, it has simply undergone transmutation so that it appears like a liquid, but in fact, it is merely transformed into a solid mass."

"Can you scan the fissure and show us what it looks like now?" asks Kaetlyn.

A hologram appears. "The depth is just over six meters, and 1.4 meters in width. As you can see, the slag has filled the entire cavity, forming a perfect seal."

"Amazing," utters Serena, who until now has just been spectating. "How long will it stay like that?"

L.I.N. smiles. "Permanently."

"Except for the ice around it, right?" says Shamus.

"Correct. At its current rate of melt, this ice will disappear in less than a year, possibly even two."

Kaetlyn lets out a sigh, frustration written all over her face. "It's like Colonel Desmond said, this entire operation is nothing more than putting a band aid over a bleeding artery. It is a temporary fix at best."

"Indeed," says L.I.N. "But a fix, nonetheless. Shall we proceed to the next coordinates?"

Tirelessly, the evolution proceeds.

Teams of engineers, oil riggers, scientists, and ground crews, in coordination with Russian military crews, operating mobile drilling rigs and diggers, dig into the ice where SEVERNUS is leaking, creating shafts which are then filled with truck after truck of slag.

The Arctic, relentless as always, contributes to the effort with brutal cold and brutally remorseless winds, none of which causes the operation to slow. If anything, it reminds everyone that the existential threat is upon them.

Estimated to take around sixty hours, the entire operation, start to finish, takes three days.

When it is done, Kaetlyn directs L.I.N. to return to Vorkuta, where they disembark and promptly collapse in the bunk beds awaiting them.

The following morning, coffee and breakfast greets them, and so does Karina Osipova, sitting in the canteen with a smile pasted on her lips.

"You will be happy to know that our scientists have measured a 28% reduction, so far, in emissions of the virus."

Kaetlyn shakes her head. "That's better than we expected."

Karina nods. "Yes, it is. If we can reach 50%, that will significantly reduce the permeation southward, and buy more time for the vaccine to be produced, distributed, and inoculated." She pauses. "I think we can safely say that we just saved a few billion people from imminent death."

44

Later that day, Karina Osipova approaches Kaetlyn as she walks along the tarmac, now freed of the necessity of a hazmat suit.

While the sky is still the prisoner of a deep cloud cover, a faint glow from the south announces that the sun is still there, waiting for its day.

"It feels good to be free of that thing, doesn't it?" says Karina.

Kaetlyn raises her face to brace the chilly wind. "It's only until you lose the simple things in life that you realize how much they mean."

"I was wondering if we might have a chat?"

"Sure," nods Kaetlyn.

Karina leads her to a nearby building with a small, but warm, lounge area. She offers her coffee, and they sit.

Karina opens with a question, "Would you be open to giving us a tour of your …" she pauses, "I mean, the alien craft?"

Kaetlyn raises a brow. "Us?"

"Several senior military officials and myself."

Kaetlyn is not surprised by the move, in fact, she has been wondering when this moment will come. She hesitates as she studies the woman across from her - an attractive, blue-eyed Russian, with sharp angular features and a crisp military uniform to match – something about her commands respect and admiration.

Karina speaks again. "I understand your reticence, so please, do not feel compelled to agree." She lightly shrugs. "For obvious reasons, we are curious. And …considering that not a single Russian has yet stepped foot aboard the craft, I thought it might be appropriate."

Kaetlyn leans forward, taking on a more serious aspect as she speaks. "You know what happened earlier, right?"

Karina nods. "I do, and I also know what happened recently in Alaska at the American base."

Kaetlyn's visage shifts noticeably showing her surprise. "That, was not supposed to be general knowledge."

Karina grins as she flicks her hand to the air. "Privacy is the victim of today's technology, Kaetlyn. We know what the Americans are up to, even though they like to think we do not."

"Then, you understand my reticence?"

"I do, and I respect it. But …" she nods towards the tarmac where Russian soldiers stand in the frigid cold guarding the alien crafts… "we have devoted thirty-three fighter jets and not less than two-hundred men and women, to ensure your security and no possibility of another attempt on your … those crafts," she smiles. "Given that we all just pulled off a critical undertaking, I would hope that your trust in our intentions is no longer in question."

Kaetlyn's head bobs as she considers her words. "I admit, you guys really did a brilliant job and who knows how many people you saved."

"It was a team effort."

Kaetlyn grins. "Yes, but our part was the easy part. We just sat there while L.I.N. waved her magic wand."

"I appreciate your sincerity, Kaetlyn. I find you to be incredibly humble for someone in such a unique situation."

Kaetlyn flicks a brow. "I'm not sure I'm being humble, so much as duty-bound."

"I think you are underselling yourself, and frankly, I admire you, I admire what you and your friends have endured, and what you just did to help my country and the rest of the world."

"Well … that's on you. As I understand it, it was the Russian engineers who dreamed up this handling."

"So, is that a yes?"

"Of course."

Karina's lips form into a wide smile. "Thank you, Kaetlyn. I do have one further question for you."

Kaetlyn waits.

"The drone ship," she points to the second, but larger ship parked on the tarmac near the other. "Has anyone entered that vehicle yet?"

Kaetlyn shakes her head. "No. According to L.I.N. it is just like a container ship, hermetically sealed, nothing more than a freighter with compartments containing the pods. Its on-board computer is paired to L.I.N. so whatever the lead ship does, the drone follows, just like a robot."

Karina is silent for a time.

"Something else on your mind, Colonel?" inquires Kaetlyn.

"Can I be frank with you?"

"If you trust me enough."

"I do trust you, Kaet."

"You barely know me."

Karina's head bobs as she struggles with her next words. She sighs. "When I first heard about you through the media channels, I had this feeling that you and I would meet."

"That's a bit weird?"

Karina smiles. "Yes, maybe, but nonetheless, I felt that we shared a common bond." She draws a breath.

"How so?"

Karina looks about the small lounge with a nervous tick in her eye. "Like you, I've had my own life-changing experience."

"How so?"

"As you may know, there are many reported sightings of UFOs in Siberia – in fact, statistically speaking, it is one of the highest areas of reported sightings in the world." She offers a tentative smile. "I was on a training exercise, several years ago, out by the Urals, when I saw a strange glow coming over the mountains at an incredible speed. And, having been trained on the military assets of my country, I knew we had nothing in our arsenal that could fly that speed. I watched it as it moved, first laterally across the sky, and then suddenly, vertically, without slowing its speed to make that angular turn. It went on for at least thirty minutes before it speared off into space. I knew I had just seen something not of this world."

She pauses.

"That changed me profoundly, Kaetlyn."

"You've never told anyone about it?"

She shakes her head. "Like the Americans, our military has followed a strict policy of denial when it comes to reported UFO sightings. No one talks about it, but when something creditable comes up, they are fast to cap it off."

"So, you didn't feel safe in talking about your experience."

Her head shakes. "I'd be benched, that is for sure, demoted to some redundant desk job where my credibility would be zero. Like the American military, no one in the Russian military wants to let the truth be known."

"What truth?"

"That we're not alone."

45

Ironically, Kaetlyn felt more like a tour guide than anything else, as she gave the Russian military brass, and their host, Karina Osipova, a tour of the ship.

At first, they were mesmerized, by the very idea that they were standing inside an alien craft, but then, as the tour progressed, Karina, acting as their interpreter, machine-gunned questions at Kaetlyn and Shamus, although, it was Kaetlyn who had to answer most of them since Shamus was not yet up to the task.

The dialogue between the highly decorated men was fast and furious, all of it in Russian, of course, but there was no question about the nature of it as their eyes fed on the inside of the craft like a mouse devouring a block of cheese.

The coup d'état was when she introduced them to L.I.N., and L.I.N. being L.I.N., proceeded to wow their minds with details about her existential skills.

From that point, the tour locked on L.I.N. as the men asked untold questions of her.

When the visit finished, and the others had left the ship, Kaetlyn asks Karina to stay behind.

"Your thoughts?" she asks with a submerged smile.

"It's mind-blowing, and L.I.N… she's just … out of this world."

"She is, literally! Anyhow, they spent a lot of time talking to her."

Karina nods. "You do realize that L.I.N. is the focus of everyone's attention. While the ship itself is incredible and no doubt, contains real gems of technology, an actual A.I. such as L.I.N. is a game-changer. And besides, she's so…"

"…human," Kaetlyn finishes her sentence.

"Yes."

Karina lingers for a time, her mind caught in another place. "What are you plans now, Kaetlyn?"

"We'll take the ships back into orbit and give everyone time to get the vaccine produced and distributed. I don't think anyone has time to talk about global warming right now, even though it's about the only thing we should be discussing."

Karina eyes the drone sitting on the tarmac in the distance. "It's hard to believe that inside that craft is the answer to global warming."

"Half the answer, Karina."

Karina flicks a brow. "Uh, yes, of course. The real battle facing us is reducing carbon emissions – and I suspect that battle is going to be bloody as hell."

Kaetlyn smiles, seeing in Karina a kindred soul of sorts.

"How about a coffee and some chocolate covered Kartoshka?"

"Kartoshka, what's that?"

"Kind of like a donut, but shaped more like a potato, which is what *kartoshka* means in Russian."

Stepping from the ship they start walking across the tarmac, when suddenly, a strange sensation permeates their bodies, like thousands of pin pricks, and as every light on the base blinks out, engulfing them in utter blackness.

A sound suddenly breaks the bizarre taciturnity.

They turn to see the ship, its engines roaring to life with a high-pitched whine.

46

"What do you mean the ships disappeared?" demands Colonel Desmond speaking over the phone to his Operations Watch Chief.

"Sir!" answers the man as he stares at a row of computer screens. "We were monitoring the Russian airbase with three different satellites. The whole base went black, like someone turned off every light. By the time the satellites reconfigured, the alien crafts were gone."

"What about Kaetlyn and the others?"

"We don't know yet."

Desmond hangs up the line and dials up Vice-Admiral Calhoon, the Irish Joint Chief of Staff, who is on the ground coordinating emergency evacuation of the populace from Dublin.

"What is it Desmond, I've got my hands full here?"

"Sir, we have a problem…" he went on to explain.

"What do you propose?"

"Reach out to the high command in Moscow and ask for a coordinated search at their end."

"Hold on," Desmond, says Calhoon as he takes another call. Moments later he returns.

"That was Sergey Grishin calling me direct."

"You mean the Russian Army General."

"The same. He claims that someone sabotaged their base and at that same time the two alien crafts took off. He also informs me that two women got on board before it took off."

Desmond feels his chest tightening. "That must have been Kaetlyn and Serena…"

"No," interjects the Admiral, "Serena is still on that base. It was the other woman, Karina Osipova."

47

"What was that?" asks Kaetlyn of L.I.N. as the ship settles into orbit around the planet in less than 60 seconds.

"An EMP, and it is safe to assume that I was its target."

Kaetlyn looks at Karina who is steading herself against one of three seats, her eyes flicking nervously back and forth between Kaetlyn and the viewscreen showing Earth passing by.

"Uhm …" she begins to answer as her eyes remain glued to the screen, "L.I.N.'s conclusion seems about right. I cannot see any other reason than sabotage."

Kaetlyn jaw tightens. "Gawd, they just won't give up."

"You think it was the Americans?" poses Karina.

Kaetlyn shrugs. "Who else. If it was your people, why sabotage their own base and force L.I.N. to evacuate the ship."

"That's logical," chimes in L.I.N.

"L.I.N., can you look around and see what you can find out? I want to know who is behind this…"

Before she can finish her sentence, L.I.N.'s voice cuts the air like a frigid knife. "There are two missiles heading our way."

48

Admiral Willis sits at his desk, his body rigid as a board with anticipation as he listens to Rockwell Sims, CEO of ADX, three thousand miles away on the other side of the country.

"The missiles just launched, Admiral," announces Sims matter-of-factly.

"And?"

"We're tracking its position now."

"Good. I have coordinated with the Admiral over the Navy. Give me the coordinates when you know where they come down, and we will have ships there as fast as possible."

49

"This ride could get very bumpy," announces L.I.N as she suddenly drops the ship from its orbital path, like a rock falling at terminal velocity.

Both Kaetlyn and Karina grip their chairs as the feeling of freefall strikes a discordant note in their stomachs.

Karina's eyes are wide with fear. "Who's shooting at us?"

"I can only tell you that they emanated from a nearby satellite," answers L.I.N as she deftly cuts a wide arc. The sudden and intensified G-forces press both Kaetlyn and Karina into their seats, as they watch two missiles streaking by the ship's front portal.

"They are locked on us," announces L.I.N. as she drops the ship even lower and arcs it on a sharp angle to avoid letting them to close.

"Can you tell what they are?" asks Kaetlyn.

"They are designed to release an electro-magnetic pulse, that much is clear."

"You have to keep us out of their range."

"Then it is best if I take us back into space."

"Just do it," screams Kaetlyn as the sudden arc of the ship sends her stomach plummeting.

"My stomach is about to explode," adds Karina.

Suddenly the ship angles to the to one side and goes into another steep dive.

"What's happening, L.I.N., why did you deviate?"

"Two more missiles were fired at us. They have us triangulated. If I try to pass between them, we will be vulnerable to the blast."

"What alternatives do we have then?"

"I can dive into the sea below, but at this speed, it will probably kill both of you," answers L.I.N.

50

The sound of vacant silence fills the void of his office as Admiral Willis waits for word.

His impatience finally takes over, "What the hell is going on, Sims?"

"Hold on… we're checking," comes the man's voice over the loudspeaker.

For Admiral Willis, the moment is titanic, a crowning one, because now, he can finally accomplish what no one else has managed to do – getting that craft in American hands. In his hands.

For Willis, a career soldier, this singular accomplishment will not only be the ultimate feather in his cap, but a turning point in history.

"Admiral," comes the voice of Rockwell Sims. "Just tell me, is it done?"

51

With four ADX-SR missiles closing in on them, and nowhere to turn without encountering one of them, L.I.N. continues the steep descent.

"What's the plan?" asks Kaetlyn, she forces the words past her lips, her jaws crimped tight as her stomach, in fact, her whole body rigidly fixed to the chair as she watches the ocean coming up at them through the viewscreen.

"I will attempt a final maneuver, in the hopes of forcing them to crash into the water."

"Assuming we don't die first."

"Have faith, Kaetlyn," says L.I.N.

Kaetlyn and Karina brace for what seems an inevitable impact, and in those final seconds, a life lived flashes before their eyes.

For Kaetlyn, it will be a repeat performance of her last life and death, aboard this very ship.

Kaetlyn grips the chair until her knuckles are white, wondering to herself if in her next life, wherever that should be, will she remember this one, or more to the point, will it haunt her too.

Suddenly, and without warning, L.I.N. pulls the ship abruptly to one side, the maneuver is so acute that the ship skids over the ocean surface, like a rock skipping across the water.

Both women clench their teeth as the G-force grinds them into one side of their chairs with a painful crunch.

"Fook!" exclaims Kaetlyn, when suddenly, her attention is distracted by a series of bright flashes in the viewscreen.

"What just happened?"

L.I.N. turns to the pale-faced ladies. "Apparently, we have a guardian angel."

Kaetlyn represses the bile lingering at the base of her throat, and then manages one word.

"What do you mean?"

"Someone intercepted those missiles."

"Show me the feedback," commands Kaetlyn, at which the view screen morphs with a clear view of what just occurred. They watch as fighter jets sweep down from the clouds at death-defying speed, their tracers lighting up the sky like fireworks as their high caliber slugs smash into the missiles, sending them crashing into the sea.

"Can you play back that footage, again?" asks Karina.

"Of course," answers L.I.N. as the holo resumes.

Karina leans closer as she watches and then

turns to Kaetlyn with a surprised look.
"Those are Russian MiGs from Vorkuta."

52

President Tamp broods over the latest news of yet another failed attempt to secure the alien crafts.

The phone next to him rings. He taps the speaker. "What?!"

"It's the President of Russia calling."

Tamp sits upright. "What?!"

"He insists on speaking to you."

Tamp sighs. *Just what I need now*, he thinks to himself, as he taps the blinking line.

"Vladimir, what can I do for you?"

The man's heavy Russian dialect bleeds through as he speaks. "Don't pretend you don't know why I call, President Tamp."

"To gloat, I assume."

A small chuckle emits from the other end.

"Whatever you think, it is wrong."

"You've changed your tune from two months ago when you tried to steal that ship from under our nose."

"Da. Two months ago we did not have pandemic. Those ships just helped save millions of my people – yours too."

"For which we are grateful."

"And yet, you still try to take it for America only."

"Do not play that card with me, Vlad. You would do the same in our situation."

"Maybe."

"So, what now?"

"I cannot let you take those crafts."

"So, you would stop us if we tried again?"

"Da."

"Why, Vlad? Why?"

The Russian President pauses before answering.

"I do not understand everything about these … Visitors. I do not understand why this girl, this Kaetlyn O'Sullivan can make claims she does, but I do know one thing now."

"Which is?"

"Whoever they are, whatever they are – we need their help."

O

1

Five weeks had passed since the antidote for Severnus, came off the production line and a massive global distribution had been initiated, a worldwide inoculation process that had no precedent in history, but then again, short of the ice age, there had never been an existential threat to all humanity, in fact, all living things, like Severnus.

Kaetlyn sits in the front row of the main hall at the *Anhembi Parque Convention Center,* in Santana, a district of São Paulo, Brazil.

On one side of her sits Shamus, and next to him, Serena. To Kaetlyn's left is Karina Osipova.

After surviving the missile attack, weeks before, the two had bonded as friends and associates with a common interest. With the grace of her commander back in Russia, who had sanctioned her extended stay aboard the alien craft, Karina was learning everything she could, and to that end, L.I.N. was the best teacher of them all.

Of course, to the Russian military it was a win-win, but to Kaetlyn, Karina was becoming the friend she never had – someone who saw the world much the same as she did.

Like Kaetlyn, Karina had been orphaned at the age of two when her parents died in a car crash outside Moscow. Raised by another family, she developed a deep sense of independence and the feeling that she never quite belonged anywhere. Coming of age, and attracted by the opportunity to advance her education, she joined the military, where, as it turns out, she became a translator, and a specialist in researching anomalies which were often reported across the vast Siberian tundra.

The Moderator, Adriana Sosa, the newly elected President of Brazil, who took office after her predecessor was forced out by public outcry, a man more interested in maintaining financial ties with China than saving the depleting Amazon rain forest, steps up to the podium and graciously addresses the forum with just a hint of her native Portuguese.

"Thank you, all, for coming to this, the *GCI*, or *Global Crisis Intervention*, a summit of …" she waves a hand around the hall, "comprised of no less than 183 of the world's leaders." She pauses. "I will be your moderator, since my country is hosting this summit, and over the course of the next two days we will come to a unilateral agreement on a strategy to stop global warming and reverse the damage done by greenhouse effect. To do so, we must first set aside our national interests, and focus on saving our planet, and our race from the disastrous effects of global warming, with its ravaging fires which have already eviscerated huge tracks of the Amazon, the Australian domain, and now southeast Asia, but also the melting polar caps, the ice tsunami which is causing a debacle along the eastern seaboard of Canada and America, and of course, Severnus – which has…" she paused, "resulted in the deaths of nearly six-hundred-million people and is expected, despite all our efforts to inoculate everyone, likely to raise that figure closer to a billion before we have effectively vaccinated much of the world. Efforts to cap-off the fissures in the Severny region of Russia, have shown success in reducing the seepage of Severnus by over 50%, which is only to say that we have bought ourselves a little more time, but we remain on Mother Nature's hit list right now, because unless we can stop the melting of our polar regions, the virus, however much remains imbedded in that icecap, will eventually be released and that threatens all living creatures, not just us. We cannot inoculate every cow, pig, or chicken we raise, and with the countless billions of dead animals in the wake of Severnus, world hunger will soon become an apocalypse of its own."

She pauses to take a sip of water. "So, with that rather sobering foreword, let me introduce our first guest speaker, one you have all heard of – and, frankly, one that no one, beyond a small handful of people, have ever met." She steps next to a metal ring on the stage.

"Please welcome, L.I.N."

Her image appears, in holographic form, but as real as if she is standing there before them. The audience is caught by surprise, as evidenced by the hushed reaction.

Standing well over two meters tall, with braids of silver hair cascading down her back, pronounced cheek bones and emerald eyes, she is a remarkable sight.

"Hello," she says with a smile. "I am L.I.N., an acronym for ***Live-Intelligence-Network***, of which I am, or at least was, when we embarked on this mission, the most advanced rendition of what you might call an Artificial Intelligence."

She steps from the circle, evoking a stir as she walks toward the edge of the platform, her eyes making contact at her gawking audience.

"Under normal circumstances, I would not be presenting myself to you, in fact, to do so violates one of our prime mandates, however, as we all know, rules must sometimes be broken."

She tips her head at Kaetlyn, who sits in the front row to one side. "As you may know, our mission to your planet, which began on the day we arrived here, nineteen years, six months and 28 days ago to be precise, involved three other members of the crew, of which two are now sitting in this audience … however, in another version of themselves." She smiles. "The details of how this came to be is another matter and not of importance to this gathering. I have been invited to present a solution to global warming – if I may?"

The Moderator nods.

"Our original mission, to prevent global warming from becoming an existential threat to you, was predicated on certain markers which showed that Earth was heading towards a threshold which would be disastrous – in fact, irreversible, if allowed to continue. The bio-bots, which you no doubt have heard of, are tiny synthetic nanorobotic devices, each one about the size of a flea. They are the delivery system for what we call the *Intervention*. They were specifically engineered to replicate the very same process that trees and other plants perform, known as photosynthesis. Each bio-bot absorbs carbon dioxide from the atmosphere, along with sunlight, and then releases it in the form non-toxic energy. In effect, these bio-bots, which are programmed to stay afloat, and are self-propelling, would continue this clean-up process until there remained no excess of CO2 emissions in the atmosphere, a maximum timespan of six years, at which point the planet's temperature should return to normal." She flashes a holo in the air next to her. "The other ship, which we refer to as the Drone, contains the delivery pods," she points to the image of one. "Each pod holds millions of these bots, and in case you were wondering, they are biodegradable, so when they do expire, they simply fall to the planet and are easily absorbed."

She steps from the stage and approaches the crowd.

"I have done many calculations, based on the current state of your planet, and that state, as you well know, has considerably worsened from twenty years ago when we first assessed global warming. You are rapidly approaching an increase in temperature of 1.6+ degrees, which is considered, as you may know, the tipping point, and why we see the disasters occurring as they are. As the planet heats up, the massive fires will continue to rage, the polar caps will continue to accelerate their melt, and there are more disasters in store. The worst is yet to come," she pauses to let that sink in. "The real existential threat is your oceans, which produce 70% of the oxygen that you and all creatures breathe, and the source of that oxygen is phytoplankton in the seas. Since 1950, the number of phytoplankton in the oceans has dropped by 40% due to whaling, commercial fishing, animal agriculture and pollution. And now, just in the past decade alone, it has dropped yet another 20%. I do not need to elucidate the point further, other than to say, that if the oceans warm and the phytoplankton disappears, so does most of your oxygen, without which you cannot survive."

One could hear a pin drop.

"As one of your more popular activists said on the subject of climate change, "Listen to the science," I too implore you to do the same. The solution which we propose will not work, however, cannot even be started unless you dramatically reduce carbon emissions first. Continued carbon emissions would hinder the process, the planet would not cool down, and the debacle which you see, would simply worsen."

"Moreover, you have already lost thousands of species, and before the virus has finished its assault, and before global warming is halted, you will lose thousands more. These species will be extinct, forever lost to your world, and so, in the end, whatever balance comes back to Earth, its ecosystem will never be as it was."

L.I.N. walks along the front row of people, her stature towering above them as their eyes are glued to her.

She draws a finger in the air, summoning another holographic image which zooms out above the group, like a giant balloon. "The current density readings of CO2 recently passed 480 ppm, parts per million, the highest carbon footprint in your atmosphere in, quite possibly, millions of years, which is trapping heat inside the atmosphere and causing the greenhouse effect." She pauses. "Let me be clear, you are not the first planet we have visited an *Intervention* upon." She nods at Kaetlyn. "This process has been done elsewhere, both successfully and unsuccessfully. In every case where it failed, the reason was the same. We did not ensure that the culture stopped its egregious and criminal abuse of the planet they depended upon, and I assure you that you cannot escape the consequences of this, unless you stop this abuse and remove the carbon emissions that are there."

She resumes her position on the center platform.

"Naturally, there are those who claim that this is all hyperbole," his gaze subtly stops on the Presidents of America and China before continuing, "however, I assure you that I am incapable of both hyperbole and falsehood, but those making such claims, have other agendas to protect, agendas that do not have your welfare in mind."

She turns to the Moderator. "Thank you, for inviting me to your forum."

"Thank you, L.I.N." responds the President of Brazil at which L.I.N.'s holographic image fades, followed by dialogue erupting from within the group.

The Moderator waits a moment before continuing. "I would like to ask that you hold all discussions until we are done with this part of the presentation." The hushed conversations fade.

"I will now ask Dr. Alaki, from the University of Central Florida, to take the stage."

Dr. Alaki, a tall, yet stooped man with a scraggly shag of hair over the lower half of his face, takes the stage and turns to the audience.

"Thank you. As L.I.N. has just described the bio-bots which they plan to release into the atmosphere, will replicate the process of photosynthesis, thus cleaning up excess carbon emissions that are there. The problem that we must face, collectively, is how to stop further toxic emissions. We, at the University of Central Florida, have been working on a solution, in fact, ironically, the answer we produced also uses artificial photosynthesis as a means of producing clean and sustainable energy, a process which can replace the outdated methods which are destroying our world."

He clicks a remote showing a diagram. "In photosynthesis, plants convert CO2 and sunlight, specifically, the violet and red wavelengths, resulting in the sugars which plants feed on. The problem we encountered in replicating this process, was how to control light so that it would trigger the CO2 into a form of reusable energy – instead of sugars. We needed something that would pick up the violet and red wavelengths of light – and the materials that can do that are expensive and scarce, such as uranium. After considerable testing, we found a substance that is inexpensive and non-toxic – which can pluck out the violet and red wavelengths of sunlight, and that is titanium. Trial and error with different combinations, countless tests, we finally devised a cocktail which included a salting of organic molecules to help in the absorption of sunlight, and bingo, we had a formula that successfully converted CO2 into solar fuel. Clean, reusable energy."

A mild hush emits from the audience.

Dr. Alaki turns to the screen and points to an image that appears.

"Meet **Hoover**," he smiles. "It's not the official designation, we just took license to use that name because it is analogous to what it does. The device you see here is a beta version, about the size of a loaf of bread, but it can be replicated in assorted sizes, small or large. On the top," he points a laser, "sunlight is absorbed through these solar cells. Air is sucked in at this end," he points, "and is mixed with the molecular cocktail containing tiny particulates of titanium and the organic material, and the resultant air exiting from this end, is clean, carbon-free air. Meanwhile, the conversion process produces reusable solar energy which is stored in a condenser, or battery, inside, and can then be transferred for use as actual power."

More sounds bubble from the audience.

"**Hoover** can be adapted for use in cars, trucks, airplanes, factories, homes, you name it. The device runs 24/7, cleaning up carbon emissions while providing more than ample energy for use in any scenario."

He turns to the audience.

"**Hoover** works. It is efficient, inexpensive to fabricate, and moreover, it can be integrated into any functionality, replacing existing use of biofuels which are killing our world."

2

As the attendees file from the hall for lunch, discussions are burning like small forest fires.

A man approaches where Kaetlyn stands with the others. A moment later he is escorting her the far corner of the mezzanine, where the Brazilian television, *Rede Globo*, the second largest commercial television network in the world, has set up to do live interviews on those at the summit, and the first ever interview of Kaetlyn O'Sullivan.

Kaetlyn had agreed to the interview – but only after Serena had coached her over the hurdles of going public – something that her introvertive nature avoided like a plague.

The interviewer, Adelina Silva reaches out a hand. "Thank you, for agreeing to this live interview," she says as she leads Kaetlyn to the set. "The interview will be short, as agreed, but it will be live and will be seen by many millions of people, not only here in Brazil, but elsewhere." She smiles. "Are you ready?"

Kaetlyn nods.

Adelina looks to camera man who raises a hand and counts down from five.

She turns to the cameras and opens the broadcast in Portuguese…

"Olá, eu sou Adelina Silva, e bem-vindo a uma edição muito especial do The Interview. Hoje, estamos no Anhembi Parque e nossa convidada especial é Kaetlyn O'Sullivan, que muitos de vocês conhecem como Star Girl".

She turns to Kaetlyn. "Thank you for being on our show, Kaetlyn."

"Thanks for having me."

"The circumstances of your being here, in Brazil, are not particularly good, are they?"

"The only good thing is that world leaders are finally facing the crisis head-on."

"How do you think the summit is progressing?"

"So far, so good, but the real challenge is coming."

"Why is that?

Kaetlyn draws a breath. "Because everyone must agree to the terms of reducing carbon emissions – that is, NZE, or Net-Zero-Emissions. It will require that every nation initiates an uncompromising evolution to shift in their infrastructure, to clean sustainable energy systems and eliminating, in a brief time, the use of fossil fuels and other systems which are causing global warming."

"Like Brazil."

"Yes."

"And you anticipate a problem getting everyone to agree, even though Severnus has already killed hundreds of millions?"

Kaetlyn shrugs. "I do. Up till now, the biggest polluters have snubbed their noses at global warming."

"What do you think should happen if a leader refuses to abide by the unilateral sanctions to achieve NZE?"

Kaetlyn fixes her eyes on the camera. "I think non-compliance to the sanctions should be treated as a criminal offense. Look at what happened because of Severnus alone. It would be pure insanity to refuse to abide by NZE, and a crime against the future of our race and the planet."

"What will you do after the summit is over?"

Kaetlyn steals a glance at Serena and Shamus who stand off to one side. "Whatever we can do to help expedite NZE so that we can move ahead with the *Intervention*."

"Which means deploying these …" she hesitates.

"Bio-bots," answers Kaetlyn.

"Right. What about the controversy over who owns the alien ships? What is your stand on that issue?"

Kaetlyn raises a challenging brow. "There is no controversy, Adelina. Those ships belong to no one except the people who sent them here."

"And… has there been any contact with them."

Kaetlyn smiles. "That is a discussion for another time."

"Will you cooperate in terms of sharing whatever technology is aboard that ship?"

"That isn't my call, and it isn't anyone else's proprietary right to claim either."

"Not even the United States, who claims rights to the ship according to the Space Treaty of 1972?"

Kaetlyn's head wags firmly. "Especially them."

"Why do you say that?"

Kaetlyn leans forward. "Imagine this scenario. You organize a team of people to go to a country to help them avoid an existential event that could wipe them out. Instead of accepting your help, they attack you and then try to claim that you and your equipment, now belongs to them. What would you say to that?"

"It would be disagreeable to me."

"Now, you understand my position on the matter."

"I'd like to ask your stance on UFOs."

Kaetlyn shrugs. "Well, that's simple enough. They exist."

"So, you believe that there has been a cover up?"

"Of course."

"Why do you think governments or military, have engaged in a cover-up, declaring most UFO sightings as a hoax?"

Kaetlyn smiles. "Do you really believe that, Adelina. That all the thousands of reported UFO sightings were simply a hoax? They were covered to stop the truth from becoming public knowledge."

"What truth?"

"These governing powers and agencies were and are afraid of what would happen to their control if they acknowledged the fact that there are other intelligent species out there, who are even more advanced than our culture. All the authoritative texts and religious paradigms would be put to question, because people would start to realize that the stories and narrative they've been told since they could walk, are not true, that we are not alone in the Universe, that the world was not exclusively created by a single God, and that maybe there are better systems out there than the current one. Believe me, they fear what would happen if they opened that door just a crack."

Adelina nods. "How do you see your life in the future?"

"I'm still processing everything that has happened to me in the last several months. Ask me when we're done with the *Intervention*."

"Why are some people so afraid of you?"

Kaetlyn stiffens. "I don't know. I am just a girl from Ireland, who happens to have remembered who she was in her last life. The fact that I make such a claim has rocked the boat in various fields, from religion to science. Religious extremists, like the man who put a bullet in my head, called me a demon – and yet," she shrugs, "I bleed just like you."

"Now, that you have seen who you were before, that is, an alien who came to our world, does that change your perception - do you see yourself as different than the rest of us?"

"Knowing the truth about who we *were* in our past lives, does not change who we *are*. If anything, it helps to clarify existence and give it more meaning."

"In what way?"

Kaetlyn pauses before answering. "When you find out that you have lived lifetime after lifetime, that you do not die and fade into an oblivious state after one life as "authorities" would have us believe, and you know it with such certainty, not a matter of belief or blind acceptance, it changes your perception of everything. I do not fear death anymore, because I know it is just a door to my next life. I am not worried about failure, because you cannot really fail as an immortal being. You start to see the bigger picture, like a gameboard, an unending theater, where we play out roles on different stages, but all of them connected by a dark curtain that makes us forget one life to the next."

"You've been quoted as saying that you don't like being referred to as ***Star girl***?"

Kaetlyn grins. "Not my favorite avatar, but I've gotten used to it."

"Is it okay with you if we use that reference?"

"Of course."

"I have one last question."

Kaetlyn nods.

"There is a story circulating that you and your co-partner in this endeavor, Mr. Shamus Maguire, shared a special bond in your previous life – is there any truth to that?"

Kaetlyn steals a look at Shamus. His face remains stoic.

"It's true – we were lovers back then."

"You have to admit, that adds a sort of romantic twist to the narrative about Star Girl, doesn't it?"

"I suppose."

"Is that still the case today – do you share those same feelings?" asks Adelina.

"Let's just say that I have no better friend in the world than Shamus Maguire."

"Thank you, Kaetlyn O'Sullivan, and good luck with the conference."

3

As the last of the attendees arrive back from lunch, the double doors of the hall slam shut with a reverberating crash, followed by the explosive staccato of gunfire that stops everyone dead in their tracks.

Turning, they see men holding snub-nosed semi-automatics at them, while two more point their guns at the security guards who are being corralled to one corner of the hall.

On the faces of every attendee the greater part of the world's leaders, is written both consternation and bewilderment.

Another series of shots explode with a concussive bark that sends everyone to their knees.

"Listen up," comes the voice, as a man steps forward and marches to the stage with an arrogant stride, his gun aimed directly at the Brazilian President who stands by the podium.

"No one moves, no one touches their cell phones, no one does a thing unless I tell you, or else …" he turns and points his gun at the person nearest to him, and unloads rounds into President of South Africa, who topples dead to the floor.

Pure shock grips the room.

"Am I clear?"

There is no sound but deathly silence.

A serpentine smile spreads across his face. "Good, now take the nearest seat to you," he commands and waits until they do so, and then steps up on the stage and motions the Brazilian President to her chair.

He turns to face them. "We are ***AoG***, the ***Army of God***."

He points with the nozzle of his weapon at the people standing at the back of the hall. “Every one of us has been licensed to kill by one of your governments. Every one of us has fought in the battlefields. Every one of us has seen more bloodshed and lost more comrades than we would like to remember, and …” he pauses, “every one of us is now dedicated to the only war that matters, and that is God’s war against you,” he sweeps the weapon at the crowd, causing many of them to cower.

“What do you want?” boldly asks the Prime Minister of Canada.

The man points his gun at him, and the crowd flinches in anticipation of yet another murder. “We are here to make sure that God’s will is not interrupted.” He tips his head, inviting the PM to speak.

“God’s will?”

“Yes,” he swings his weapon in the air with a cavalier flourish. “What you are witnessing now, what is happening all around us, is God’s will. He has ordained that our time has ended, the Apocalypse is now upon us. We have been judged for our sins.”

For a moment there is silence as people are too afraid to speak up, but then another voice hushes through the thick silence, this time from the Nigerian President. “You just killed my friend, how is that God’s will? What God do you serve?”

The shooter steps from the stage, walking along the front row of people, the nozzle of his gun idly passing by their heads with casual indifference, until he comes to a stop in front of the Nigerian leader. He grins. "I serve the one true God, and as to your friend, he got what he deserved, as will all of you soon enough."

He turns to eye the blanched and terror-filled faces of those watching him. "We are not terrorists. We are ambassadors of the Lord. We are here to save you all from yourselves. God…" he points his gun to the ceiling, "has deliberated the fate of our world. Once before, for forty days and forty nights, he cleansed it of our sickness, and now he is doing it again."

"So, you plan to prevent us from trying to fix the world – that's your idea of saving it?" comes another voice from the back of the hall.

The man scans the room. "Who said that, stand up!" he commands.

Kaetlyn rises from her chair.

"Ah, the antichrist herself," his words seethe. "I have been wanting to meet you for some time, Kaetlyn O'Sullivan," he says as he walks with a measured stride toward her. "You are the harbinger, the messenger of the Apocalypse."

Kaetlyn shakes her head, emboldened by a passion burning deep inside. "I doubt that."

He waves his gun at her. "Oh, you are, you are the one who started the dominoes falling, you are the one who catalyzed all of this."

"I'm trying to fix the world, unlike you."

Angered by her boldness, he lets off a series of shots which crash into the ceiling high above. "No! You are the antithesis of good, you are the ambassador of Satan himself, a demon who works to dissuade these souls from the true path of God, by telling them lies and fabrications about how they can change a world they neither made nor have the right to fix. This is God's creation, it is his world to change, or destroy – not yours.'"

Kaetlyn's reckless passion has taken its grip on her. "It's people like you," she continues, "who has screwed up this world with your crazy ideas, your delusions and your egotistic bull…"

The man screams as loud as the bark of his next shot which crashes into the wall behind her, so close to her head that Kaetlyn recoils.

The silence that ensues is deafening.

4

The entire summit was being televised live to the world, so of course, the moment the hostage crisis begins, hundreds of millions around the globe are watching it unfold.

“What do they want?” asks Captain Marquis of the São Paulo PD as he speeds toward the convention center.

“There are no demands,” responds his Division Chief.

“Can we open a dialogue with them?”

“There is no one to talk to. They’re inside and no one is coming out.”

Marquis grits his jaw. *The most important meeting of the decade, decades, and these extremists had to pick his watch to make a stand.*

“Clear the area of civilians. I want a total lock down for at least a two-block radius. I will be there in minutes with more reinforcements.”

5

With the evacuation of the populace now done, which is only to say that they had managed to ferry or fly the swell of humanity that fled for their lives, to the Continent, the Irish emergency response teams and military had begun a massive clean-up effort, systematically identifying the dead, removing bodies, and taking them to centers to be incinerated.

The dead were identified with fingerprints only, other than that, the focus was on removing the carnage which was itself a massive health hazard.

It is a horrifyingly grotesque scene, as they work their way through the cities and towns, street by street, house-to-house, building after building, locating the dead – their bodies now bloated and in different states of decay and horribly disfigured by the virus.

The human death toll notwithstanding, they are also faced with countless hundreds of thousands, if not millions, of dead animals of every kind – the carcasses of which are also putrefying. The animal carcasses are piled up in nearby fields and burned – creating a pall of black smoke that hangs over the land for days.

The stench of death permeates the air like a thick soup.

Most of those who had not perished in the maws of Severnus, had been relocated, a massive undertaking involving every single boat and plane that could be mustered, private, military, commercial, including a literal fleet of ships sailing in from the European continent to help move a nation of souls who stood on the southern shores of Ireland and outside Belfast in the north, gripped by both a brutal winter wind, and the consternation over the advancing virus.

No one knows the death toll yet, but estimates put it at over four million, out of a population of just 6.5 million in Ireland alone.

Colonel Desmond has been working tirelessly, taking three-hour periods of sleep, and then working fourteen-hour shifts, and then collapsing yet again on a cot in the field hospital set up at the *Aviva Sports Stadium* in Dublin.

Sitting with his elbow fixed to a small table and his head resting in the palm of his hand, and a cold cup of tea, he closes his eyes and takes a moment to enjoy the bite of a chilly winter wind – and not the feeling of claustrophobic asphyxiation living inside a hazmat suit for weeks – moreover, the constant concern that a slight tear or rip could end his life.

His mobile buzzes. "Desmond here," he answers.

"When?" he exclaims as his exhausted body is suddenly catalyzed into action by the shocking news.

6

Leaving the hall, with explosives rigged to every exit, the AoG place themselves strategically throughout the main lobby of the convention center, where they can watch every exit and every ingress point.

Inside the meeting room, nerves are at a breaking point as everyone sits there, sweat pouring down their faces as they wait, facing, it seems, an inevitable and imminent death.

The British PM, seated in the front row, turns to the group. “We can’t just sit here.”

“And do what, storm the doors? He told us that any attempt to open them would set off all the explosives,” answers someone.

More discussions break out as the panic rapidly escalates to a fever pitch.

“You’re a military person, what do you think?” asks Shamus of Karina Osipova, who is busily studying the entire room for any other way out.

She answers. “If they’ve rigged explosives on every exit, it would be suicidal to attempt an escape that way, but …”

“But what?” he asks.

Her eyes drift up to the skylights high above. “If we could get up there, we could definitely break through the glass and escape.”

“But how do we do that?” asks Kaetlyn.

Karina stands and walks the entire perimeter of the hall and finally stops. She motions them over. “Here,” she points. “If we can scale this rib,” referring to a steel structural support, “we could get to that catwalk there,” she points high above. “Once someone gets on the roof, we should be able to catch the attention of the emergency response people without alerting the terrorists…”

"And then what?" asks Serena, wide-eyed with fear.

Karina shrugs. "Then we hope for the best."

Serena's eyes scan the high ceiling above. "So, someone has to climb up that beam."

Shamus shucks his light jacket. "Aye, that'll be me," he announces.

"You sure?" asks Kaetlyn with a concerned look.

He grins. "Two years ago, I was the top gymnast in our school. Used to scale ropes and all. This," his eyes wander upwards, "piece of bloody cake."

"What about the cameras?" says Kaetlyn.

Karina shakes her head. "We have to assume that they can't see us – otherwise we'd probably be dead by now," she finishes with a flick of her brow. "So…" her eyes look upward, "up you go, laddie."

7

The man, whose attire would never have betrayed his true agenda, wearing a baseball cap, t-shirt, jeans, and a pair of Nikes, stands off to one side of the mezzanine, with a clear view of the entire lobby below, while his team, eight men and two women, who are situated at strategic points below, guard all the doors.

A smile creases his lips as he glances out the window of the convention center – where clusters of police, in riot gear, SWAT teams, military tanks and soldiers – have formed a literal wall around the center.

In his hand is the dead man's switch. A piece of duct tape keeps his thumb pressed to the device preventing an accidental release, but, with a simple motion, and when the time is right, he will simply tear away the tape and send everyone to a better place, himself included.

He feels a deep sense of pride and commitment to the task at hand – all, as he continues to assert to himself and the world, in the service of the Lord.

Posing as tourists, cleaners, and catering personnel, they had carefully scouted the convention center weeks before, when news had been announced of the imminent Summit. They had painstakingly snuck in the explosives piece by piece, including the weapons, cleverly disguised, and hidden, all of it just waiting for their moment – a moment which presented itself on this very day, when over 95% of the world's top leaders were sitting in just one room.

After serving two terms in Afghanistan, he had returned to his home, in Cape Town, South Africa, a victim of PTSD, disillusioned and utterly depressed about the world, and certain that the war he had just fought had served absolutely no purpose whatsoever other than to gratify the privileged, the rich and the entitled, and to fill the bank accounts of those that war served best.

In the months that followed his return to a "normal" life, his world was broken, he was broken, and his will to live had all but expired.

At the lowest ebb, where he had nothing left to live for, constantly haunted by the visions of his friends, soldier all, ripped apart by bullets and explosives, the pain and guilt of survival syndrome stalking him like the specter of a demon, he found God.

The revelation came to him like a bolt from above, and with it came his new purpose to serve the Almighty and none other.

With that epiphany soon morphed a plan for restitution, and a passion to take back what had been stolen from him and his comrades in the deserts of that god-awful war-torn land. It had taken several years to grow a small following of zealous adherents, but they were some of the best soldiers he had ever fought with, and each of them were disenchanted former military veterans, like himself, each suffering the same PTSD, and moreover, each of them licensed to kill, people who had dedicated themselves to the new army, the AoG, the Army of God.

He grins, calling up the pained look of agony and shock in the face of the President of South Africa, the man he had shot in cold blood just an hour before.

The choice had not been by accident – *payback is a bitch,* he muses aloud, with a serpentine smile. The man had played a role in sending him and thousands like him, to war, to fight an ill-defined cause called "terrorism" – when in fact, it was just an excuse to invade a foreign land and gain a foothold – or to fill someone's accounts if only by nurturing the machinery of war.

He forces himself from his mental maundering and tips his head to the radio perched on his shoulder. "How's it going?"

"Quiet down here," answers his team leader.

"Okay, won't be long now," he says.

He watches through the window as tanks arrive and as a covey of soldiers position themselves.

"Good," he utters, *"bring them all - soon you'll see how a real army fights for God."*

8

As Captain Marquis watches the short video segment, yet again, the one posted to social media half an hour earlier, it shows a man with his weapon slung over one shoulder as he calmly announces to the world the imminent fate of their leaders and warns that any attempted incursion will automatically set off explosives rigged at all points of entry and exit in the large center.

Marquis rubs his temples, feeling the incipient migraine.

Someone approaches him as he sits in his squad car.

"Sir," the officer points to the building.

Marquis follows his finger and sees what it is. A man is standing on the roof of the building, waving at them.

"Marquis pulls the binoculars to his eyes and studies the scene more closely.

He turns to his deputy. "Get word passed to every unit, no one makes a move, no one even blinks an eye at the fact that that man is standing there. If those terrorists find out that someone has escaped, they will blow the place up. Get it?"

The deputy nods.

Marquis then radios the SWAT team leader. "Get me ten of your best people and meet me on the back side of the convention center, near…" he pauses to look at the building blue schematic, "exit twenty-three. Bring a lot of rope."

9

Marquis and his team take the service stairs leading to the roof, and moving with stealth, they are soon crouched on the open skylight, next to Shamus.

"Glad to see you blokes," says Shamus with a wide smile.

"This is how you got up?" Marquis points through the skylight.

Shamus points, "I shimmied that girder."

Marquis nods to the team leader and within seconds they have secured ropes to the roof and drop them down through the opening.

"Be careful of the cameras," says Shamus.

"We know where the cameras are, we put most of them there for security purposes," answers Marquis as the SWAT team leader disappears through the opening and rappels downward, hitting the floor in just seconds.

Fortunately, Karina, being more military minded and certainly more cool-headed than anyone else in that room, had already passed word to all the attendees, to remain seated and not to draw any attention to what was happening above.

Filled with fear, anticipation and panic, the attendees sit there, trying to appear normal, a nearly impossible task considering the fate that faces them all if this operation fails.

Several more men hit the floor and position themselves along the perimeter, careful not to be expose themselves to the cameras facing the main hall.

Within minutes, ten men and women, armed and geared to the nines, are position by two of the side exists, studying the explosives rigged to each door.

The team leader speaks into his radio to Marquis who remains above with Shamus.

"I don't see any way they have these doors rigged to go off automatically. They are bluffing."

"Are you sure?" responds the captain.

"Yes."

"Then proceed."

A vagrant motion catches the attention of one of the AoG people outside. He leans into his radio. "Something's happening in the hall," he announces.

Just then comes the explosion, as the northeast exit disappears in a cloud of smoke and debris. The explosion rocks the convention center, sending a discursive ripple throughout the structure.

"Move in, and shoot anyone that comes through that opening," commands the AoG leader as he rips away the tape holding his thumb to the detonator.

Within seconds, his people are engaged in combat with the SWAT team.

The shooting crescendos, choking the air with the ear-rupturing reports, back and forth, as the cacophony of high caliber slugs rip the air like an orchestral bedlam.

The man grins. This is everything for which he had hoped. The Army of God fighting the despotic and hypocritical forces of the sinners.

He watches, perched by the railing above, as his people desperately fight back with heart and soul, pouring a literal storm of death into the opening, and one by one, as they begin to fall, as lead tears into their flesh, cutting them open and spilling their blood to the floor in pools of red, and as the police force systematically advances.

He knows now, and he certainly knew it when this day began, as did they all, that when they committed to this duty, no one would be walking away alive.

They had each reconciled themselves to the fact that for their service to the Lord, they would walk in his light, but not this light, not after today.

The last man standing below, his team leader in fact, boldly walks toward the soldiers who press toward him, unleashing a hail of death, shredding his body until he is left convulsing in the throes of imminent death.

The AoG is gone – but its message will be remembered forever, he thinks, as his thumb, now tiring of holding the trigger down, yearns to be released of its task.

Suddenly, a horrendous crash startles him.

He looks up to see the opposite wall of the convention center disintegrating into thousands of pieces as something cuts through it like a hot knife through butter.

The moment is so surreal and so shocking, as he watches the object streaking at him, like a massive torpedo, and in that hesitation, the nanoseconds between the realization that he is about to be eviscerated by it, he decides to release his thumb; but the moment is a moment entirely too late, and like an elephant suddenly stepping a massive foot on a single blade of grass, every bone of his body is crushed as the object spears through him and then into the adjacent wall of the building, sending an ocean of material flying into the air, like paper confetti, as it spears upward into the air.

10

As Kaetlyn, Karina, Shamus, and Serena emerge, with the other attendees, into the sunlight, and the welcoming arms of emergency response teams, she turns to look at the building, where a massive hole has been cut through it – as if a torpedo had entered from one side and exited the other. She smiles.

The summit had summarily ended before anyone could come to any final agreements about how to proceed with handling global warming.

And understandably, no one is in any condition to sit in a closed space and discuss anything at that time.

An hour later, after questioning by local police, the four are standing at the far end of the parking lot, surrounded by a ring of police and military personnel, waiting as the ship descends and lands amidst a sea of castoff and debris.

Once inside, L.I.N. promptly takes the ship back into orbit without asking permission to do so.

She turns to the four, "Your vitals show that you are all quite stressed and dehydrated," announces L.I.N.

"Yeah, well, you try living through that shite-storm," says Serena with a shake of her head. "God, my life used to be simple, calm, and predictable. Now …"

"Got any beer up here?" asks Shamus.

"Unfortunately, not," answers L.I.N. "However, the drink, which you refer to as the "green goop" will hydrate your bodies much better than beer.

"Obviously, you have no appreciation of the finer aspects of our culture."

"How did you know?" asks Kaetlyn.

"You mean, how did I know which man to target?"

Kaetlyn nods.

"I didn't at first. I scanned the building and detected the explosives. My scan then picked up this one man, apart from the general fray, holding a device. It seemed reasonable to assume that he was the greatest threat."

"But, how did you even know we were in trouble?" asks Kaetlyn.

"Oh, for that you must thank Colonel Desmond."

Kaetlyn raises a questioning brow.

"I was performing routine checks on the ship, while in orbit on the other side of the planet, and quite out of touch with the entire crisis that was unfolding."

"What did he do?"

"He pinged me."

"Pinged you?"

L.I.N. nods. "Yes. He aimed one of their military satellites at me and pinged me. It caught my attention right away, so I contacted him only to find out what was happening."

"Well, I'm glad you did what you did," says Serena. "Now, how do I get some of that green goop?"

O

1

The next several weeks were tumultuous to say the least, as governments around the globe continued to pour every possible resource into producing, distributing and inoculating its citizenry against Severnus, which was still advancing, however slowly, from the Arctic region, and as teams of engineers and scientists worked tirelessly to locate even more fissures, small or large, where Severnus was still seeping into the atmosphere, in order to plug them up.

As the advancing virus continued its assault against humanity, it was becoming brutally real to both the politicos and the public at large, that global warming was not going away.

For the first time in modern history, the machinery of information – that is, social media et al., was speaking the same language – the truth.

No one was casting racial aspersions at anyone.

No one was talking about the "Islamic threat" and terrorism as a global menace.

No one was threatening war.

In fact, mention of conflicts, warring factions, murders, criminal activities, and to the wonder of most, gossip about celebrities and their sexual escapades, had waned to nothing.

Suddenly, scientists who were reporting on the situation, were in the spotlight.

Those who had casually, or even arrogantly dismissed global warming as a hoax, were now slithering in the shadows, licking their wounds, trying their best to make people forget about their assertions otherwise.

Mother Nature was now center stage, and her message was clear – *fix my planet, or else!*

The most alarming fact, one that recently took the world by a storm, was when a team of scientists in Greenland, and another in the Antarctic and yet a third in Ecuador, released their collective studies, showing conclusively that planetary temperature increase was nearly at the 1.6 threshold – and like the panic that set in over the Millennium, when world computers were expected to crash the cultural theaters, the panic over this news was exponentially off the charts.

A 1.6 increase in global temperatures was considered the breaking point.

During this time, Kaetlyn had taken the opportunity to visit her parents who were still living in temporary lodging in Belgium.

Like millions of displaced souls, from the British Isles to Scandinavia, who were temporarily sheltered in emergency camps all over Europe, her parents were anxious to get back to Bantry and resume their lives – but until military and emergency teams had cleared away the rampant death littering the cities, towns, and countryside, no one was going anywhere.

Now, weeks after the attack in São Paulo, Kaetlyn sits in the silence of the ship, her eyes following the gentle sweep of Earth in the portal. It is a sight that still mesmerizes her, with its grace and beauty, as if a Universal artist had painted it against a mantle of deep black space.

She sighs. She misses Serena who had left the ship two weeks ago, to Germany, to provide her services as a trauma counsellor to victims there.

Shamus had also left, returning to Ireland to help with the emergency clean up.

Her only company now, beyond that of L.I.N., is Karina Osipova, whom she invited to stay on for a while longer.

Karina had graciously accepted the offer, of course, with the blessings of her senior officer back in Moscow.

Karina breaks the silence. "What will you do when this all over?" she asks.

Kaetlyn shrugs. "Da' know."

Karina smiles, having developed a sensitivity for the nuances of Kaetlyn's body language.

"I think you don't want to go back to Ireland."

Kaetlyn raises an eye to her. "What makes you say that?"

"A feeling, the same one I have."

"You mean, you don't want to go back to Russia?"

"I don't want to go back to the life I was living."

Kaetlyn smirks. "You think this life is better?"

Karina flicks a hand at the screen. "Admittedly, this is a bit boring, sitting here and waiting, but in a more general sense, the prospects it presents for me are amazing."

Kaetlyn reflects on her words for a moment before speaking. "Why did you agree to stay aboard? Was it personal or do you have orders from the Kremlin to soak up everything you can and report back?"

Karina shakes her head. "Still don't trust us, uh?"

"Can you blame me, after everything we've been through?"

"No, but can you blame my government for trying to find out everything they can about all of this …" she waves a hand around. "It is, in all probability, the greatest wonder of the world, ever."

Kaetlyn sighs. "I know. And I hate to sound so dismissive or paranoid."

"I do not think you're being dismissive or paranoid, Kaet. You have been through hell, over two lifetimes, actually.” She grins. “Killed, and then shot again, and then shot at over and over – I mean, who the hell wouldn’t be a little suspicious after all that?” She pauses. “Anyhow, the answer to your question is that I am here for personal reasons, but of course, my superiors are interested in anything I can provide them.”

“And have you, have you provided them with information.”

Karina smiles. “Nothing more than what you and L.I.N. have let me in on.”

L.I.N. pipes in. “I can confirm what Ms. Osipova is saying. I have, as you know, been monitoring all communications in and out of this ship. Karina is telling the truth.”

“Thanks for the confirmation, L.I.N. So, what’s the personal flip?”

Karina’s eyes sweep over the console and then back to Kaetlyn. “The first time I stepped inside this ship, when you gave us the tour at our base in Vorkuta, I felt something come alive inside me. I had not felt that kind of animation, that kind of energy or enthusiasm since I was a young girl. Like a spark had been lit, and ever since then I have had this burning passion, a feeling that I have found my niche.”

Kaetlyn tips her head with an inquiring eye. “Your niche?”

Karina smiles. "Yes …" she pauses, feeling the temperature of the water before proceeding, "this feels like what I should be doing with my life."

2

For obvious reasons, the 2nd Summit on Global Warming, could not be held anywhere above the 50th parallel, now referred to as TZ, or the *Toxic Zone* – certainly not until the emergency teams had cleared away the death and devastation brought about by Severnus.

This included a substantial portion of Canada, Scandinavia, northern France and Germany, the British Isles, and a large part of Siberia. The worst hit areas were Mongolia and China, where winds swept the virus across the Siberian tundra. It was estimated that over three hundred million people had perished from the virus in those areas alone – but no one knew for sure, not until the final body count was in.

Rhodes, a small Grecian Island in the Aegean Sea, just a stone's throw from western Turkey, had never seen a gathering of this nature, as government planes, and chartered flights, arrived, and a line of military and police vehicles waited to whisk them off to The Best Western Plus Plaza in the center of Rhodes.

Hundreds of security personnel had already established a safe perimeter in and around the center, forming a literal blockade that is impossible for anyone to break through, and every ingress point to the island itself, is also being guarded.

By the time Kaetlyn, Shamus, and now Karina, who had become part of the entourage, arrived to the symposium, they were escorted by a military detail to a smaller, yet, adequate facility, where, once again, leaders from most every country were seated, listening, as someone updated them on the current status of global warming, including the newest devastation, the ice tsunami, a towering wall of ice, the result of the melting icecaps in the north, heading along the northeastern coast of Canada and the USA, destroying countless harbors, thousands of private and commercial ships and laying waste to coastal communities, like some behemoth from the underworld.

They settle in the back row, hardly noticed by the constituents, nor even the Moderator, the newly elected President of Greece, the first woman to ever hold the seat and herself a staunch supporter of efforts to stop global warming.

After the scientific deliverance is completed, the Moderator calls for a break.

The general mood, as leaders shuffle into the lobby to refuel, is tense.

After the hostage crisis in São Paulo weeks before, everyone is on edge and looking over their shoulders.

The President of Greece notices them sitting there. She approaches Kaetlyn. "I am sorry, we didn't know you would be attending. I would have made front row seats available for you."

"We didn't want to make it public knowledge that we were coming, for obvious reasons," answers Kaetlyn.

"I understand. I am glad you came. We need all the moral support we can get."

Kaetlyn notices two of the lingering attendees, recognizing the Presidents of China and America engaged in a private discourse."

"Do you think they will agree to the new sanctions?" she asks as she tips her head at them.

The Grecian President raises a brow, trying to maintain a diplomatically acceptable face as she answers. "To be honest, I think we're still in for a real fight."

"Hope you've got your boxing gloves on," adds Shamus with a grin.

She smiles at him. "How do you think I got to be the first female President of Greece? I haven't taken them off since the day I announced my candidacy." She winks.

When the conference begins again, it rapidly ramps up to a heated discussion – because now, the sanctions, the new rules, the new energy platforms, all of it, where the rubber meets the road, is the center of discussion.

The President, and Moderator, introduces Dr. Alaki, and his team.

Although Alaki had presented his case at the earlier conference, his model for clean renewable energy had since caught the spotlight, center stage of the media.

Their presentation, which covers forty-five minutes, is compelling as he delivers a credible model for accomplishing Net-Zero-Emissions within 24 months, using the development he had earlier introduced as Hoover, but which they have since renamed, CEPO – an acronym for ***Clean-Energy-Prduction-Unit*** – a modular unit that runs clean, leaves absolutely no carbon footprint, absorbs carbon emissions as it provides energy, and can replace all existing energy infrastructural systems.

Without ado, the Prime Minister of Sweden stands and starts the dominos falling by committing his country to the sanctions without question. He is followed by the Chancellor of Germany, the Canadian and British PMs, the President of Finland, Estonia, Italy, on and on. It seems that across the boards, so far, there is little resistance, but of course, those nations which account for 60% of the greenhouse gas emissions, are as silent as a mute.

The Moderator finally turns an eye to the President of the United States with an expectant aspect.

President Tamp draws a deep breath as he realizes that he is now forced to make his stand – a position he has not faltered on over the past months.

"I've listened to everything that has been presented, and I've discussed this matter at length with members of my Administration, and despite the circumstances, it is our position, my position, that we cannot agree to unilateral sanctions as presented here. If we were to impose the 24-month mandate on all industries in America, we would be facing a corporate meltdown, and a recession, or worse, as the backbone of America pours its resources into changing its entire infrastructure to comply to these sanctions. Such a move, in fact, could be more disastrous to us than simply dealing with the progressive effects of global warming in the best way we can."

There was no holding back the wave of emotional responses that clipped his statement, and at that moment the Moderator watches on as the Summit veers off the road, like a car suddenly plummeting over a cliff, as attendees launch a heated assault at the American leader.

3

“Geez… that went well,” jokes Shamus as the Summit, now officially a political shit-show, breaks once again for coffee and snacks, although, it appears more like a time-out to let tensions deflate.

Kaetlyn shakes her head. “What is it with the Yanks? I mean, why do they feel so self-entitled?”

Shamus shrugs as he pours a cup of coffee for them, grabs some muffins, and leads her to a distant table, away from the crowd.

“It is not about Americans, Kaet. I imagine it is a very divided camp in America when it comes to the issue of global warming. The real problem is Tamp, is a narcissistic, pompous, and self-serving man, if I am honest. Tamp does not serve “the people.” He serves the oligarchy, the corporate and financial hegemony that really is in charge in America. Like L.I.N. said earlier, it is an elitist class of very wealthy people who are only interested in maintaining control and who hijacked the political system of America decades ago to make sure that they never lose that control.” He pauses to ingest a muffin. “Sadly, Americans think they have a democracy, but they don’t anymore, they are ruled by an oligarchical class – and Presidents, like Tamp, empower them.”

Kaetlyn tips her head at him. “Pretty deep stuff.”

"Well, if you must know, I was planning to major in political sciences." He flicks a brow. "Now, I'm not so sure what the hell I'm gonna do after this shite-show."

She smiles. "Everything is up in the air, isn't it?"

"You could say that. I mean, how do you a plan a future when the world is on the brink?"

Kaetlyn sighs. "I know. Until this is all over, I try not to think about it."

4

Two hard long days into the Summit, with most nations now aboard and agreed to the unilateral sanctions for NZE, three nations are still arguing in favor of less stringent sanctions and are holding out. And given that these nations are the prime contributors to the greenhouse effect, the Summit is at a stalling point, like a plane about to nosedive.

Tiring of the discussions, the back-and-forth play, the theatrics of it all, Kaetlyn and Karina finally return to the ship, extremely happy to get away from all of it, while Shamus jumps a flight back to Ireland to continue helping there.

Kaetlyn sips on a hot cup of tea, having stashed some aboard the ship as an alternative to the goop which L.I.N. insists is better for their health and well-being.

She watches as the Italian peninsula roles by, her head shaking.

"You're disappointed," says Karina.

Kaetlyn turns to her.

"Aren't you?"

"I am not as invested in this as you are, Kaet. And besides, my skin is a bit thicker than yours, having spent five years in the Russian military. That …" she waves a hand to the air, "is a tough crowd."

"In what way?"

"Communism may have officially disappeared in our nation back in 1989, but I can tell you that its vestiges are still threaded in the mentality of those who run the military. Tight-lipped, unchallengeable authority, do what command says, you know, not exactly a place for freethinkers like you and I."

"And yet, you stayed with them. Why?"

Karina shrugs. "I guess I was waiting for something better to come along."

Kaetlyn resumes staring out the portal. "My lack of life-experience is making me naïve about all of this. In my head, it simply makes sense to agree to unilateral sanctions to save the planet, but obviously, other forces prevail than logic." Her head wags as her disgruntlement paints a picture on her face. "America pulled out of the Paris Climate Accord two years ago and put itself first – even though they are one of the two worst contributors to global warming. China has taken little action to stop their murderous pollution which renders entire cities almost unbreathable. Iran and the Saudis will not let go of their oil cash cow – even though they are fueling the debacle. And then, there's Russia…" she pauses to look Karina in the eyes."

Karina grins. "Don't worry, I'm not offended, and I'm not so nationalistic as to be blind to weaknesses of my own country. As hard as it is to accept, Kaet, the economies of these nations, which constitutes over two billion people alone, are so entrenched and dependent on the current energy systems, that to change them, despite the global threat, is, in their eyes, more destructive."

"I get the mentality - I just don't get the logic."

"There is no logic here. These are short-sighted men – with short-sighted aims. Tamp is an enabler – that is all. If he really cared about America, he would not be resisting NZE. Same with the Chinese regime – they have each have their own agendas and it has truly little to do with the welfare of their people and more to do with ensuring the right people, the right establishment, remains in power even when they leave office."

Kaetlyn sighs. "All this talking, and no action, is just giving global warming a bigger head start. How do we compel them to see past their short sightedness and grasp the bigger picture?"

L.I.N. appears in front of them. "May I offer a suggestion to you ladies?"

Kaetlyn shrugs.

"If you may recall, some months ago, when our ship was first discovered, and your part in that story had been revealed to the Americans and the Irish, you were, as I remember, in a very difficult and yet, somewhat similar position."

Kaetlyn raises an eye to her holo. "Go on."

"You were sitting on an American aircraft carrier, their largest in fact, while the Irish and the Americans argued over possession rights, and you were becoming increasingly concerned about how to stop our vessel from becoming the victim of yet another attempt to hide the greater truth from the world."

Kaetlyn's eyes drift idly for a moment as she recalls the moment.

She turns to L.I.N. "That's bloody brilliant."

5

"What do you mean, 'She's live?'" demands President Tamp, as he bolts upright from his hotel bed, fumbling with the television remote as he does.

"See for yourself, she's on every major network, CNN, CBS, BBC, you name it," answers his Chief of Staff in Washington.

"How is that even possible?"

"Who knows. Somehow, she hijacked the networks."

Tamp manages to turn on the BBC channel and watches with a gritted jaw as her face appears on the television.

"… I recently left the Summit on climate change, which is still on-going in Rhodes. Most leaders have agreed to the sanctions for Net-Zero-Emissions, but unfortunately, several nations are holding out, specifically, America, China, Iran, and the Saudis, who are refusing to agree to those sanctions, claiming that to do so would result in economic collapse for them." She pauses. "I know that you have probably heard many things about me, some of them strange, unbelievable, maybe even a bit scary, but what you need to know is that I am one of you. I grew up here, just like you. I was raised by two wonderful people in Ireland. I went to school, drank beer, and watched Netflix. Where I came from before now is another story and is not important. What is important, right now, is what we can do with the resources we have." Her eyes fix on the camera. "I am appealing to you, the American people, the people of China, the Iranian people, and the rest of the world – it is time for you to make a stand and for YOU to take back control of YOUR future. Right now, every day spent in discussions, every minute lost arguing over these sanctions, is a minute where more people are dying, thousands of them, where species are disappearing forever, where you and your families, your children, and their children, will be threatened with that extinction. Mother Nature is making an assault against us, and she is not going to stop until we stop attacking her. I am not asking you to revolt or to resort to violence. I do not want you to go out and burn flags or start fires or anything like that. I am appealing to your principles and to your sense of what is right, to make a final and definitive stand against the forces which are threatening us all. Do not ask your leaders for permission anymore, it is your world. It your life. It is your future. We have waited long enough for the leaders of our world to act. Most are trying, but unfortunately, some have been compromised to such a degree that they answer to others, and those agendas do not include the welfare of you, your children or even their grandchildren." Kaetlyn pauses to take a deep breath. "I am asking you to stand up and DEMAND that those sanctions be unilaterally approved and put into motion NOW. If they are, and if they are stringently followed, starting now, it is possible, based on the projections of scientists, that within 24 months we can do our part and reverse the climatic disaster facing us all. This is not fake news, this is fact, based on scientific studies by scientists around the globe. There is no question about the future facing you and your children. It will only get worse, and in time, it will become an existential event threatening everyone and every living thing." Her face remains dour. "Your children deserve a chance to make a better world – don't take it away from them. Put the world first. Put the children before money. Net-Zero or nothing"

6

The Summit resumes the following morning, and discussions continue, both heated and otherwise, as President Tamp, his Chinese counterpart, the Iranian President, and representatives of the Saudi conglomerate, dig in their heels against the proposed unilateral sanctions on Net-Zero-Emissions.

By mid-afternoon, however, the tune changes as the media reveals a startling event unfolding across the globe.

From Europe to the British Isles, America to China, the Middle East to the southern extremities of New Zealand, Russia, in fact, most every nation, people are walking off their jobs, and amassing in public squares.

A literal ocean appears in Washington, marching up The Mall, while hundreds of thousands of Chinese pour into Tiananmen Square in Beijing – the same picture repeating all around the world with placards and chants taken right from Kaetlyn's global transmission…

Put the world first!
Put children before money!
Net-Zero or Nothing!

By the end of the day, schools across the world are closing, not because anyone in authority ordered it, but because the teachers and the students alike, have walked away and joined the movement in their local towns and cities.

Airlines ground to a halt in most every city as pilots joins in – sending global travel into a spiraling nose-dive.

Every avenue in the culture joins the march.

By the end of the day, it is the largest global protest ever recorded in history, as the wheels of society come to a blistering stop, and the people make their stand.

And on that day, the Rhodes Summit concludes.

O

1

Twenty-one months had passed, during which time the wheels of change brought about revolutionary shifts in the global energy infrastructure.

Those most resistive to making the necessary changes, because of the *Rhodes Summit* and *NZE*, now unilaterally mandated by law, was primarily the oil and the car manufacturing industry, and those engaged in production of military arsenals, who stood to lose the most.

Regardless of protests, automakers were given six months to introduce new engine systems based on clean technology – or what the industry had dubbed CETS – *Clean-Energy-Technology-Systems.*

Failure to comply meant facing immediate criminal charges. No trials. No jury. Just a conviction.

Car owners were required to get their vehicles re-outfitted and re-certified within 18 months, in conformation with CETS.

The oil companies who harvested the blood of the Earth, screamed like petulant children, threatening to crash the market with inflated oil prices, but nothing they said or did came near to what Mother Nature was already unleashing, so no one bothered to listen to their rant. They were shown the new sanctions, given the same timelines to meet, and faced the same criminal charges for failure to comply. Eventually, it was simply too painful to scream anymore.

Every industry, to one degree or another, was affected by NZE.

Every household, every human being, in fact, was feeling its effects as markets shook, as the very infrastructural stanchions of the world trembled, and yet, surprisingly, nothing critical collapsed as naysayers and doomsday zealots claimed would happen. And the reason for that was simple – the people wanted it, and the people were the ones keeping the boat afloat despite the holes letting water in.

For the first time in the history of this world, the power of the people was demonstrably and unilaterally more than the people in power – and this dynamic itself was changing the ideological and political paradigms which had dominated the mentality of the world for so long.

2

L.I.N. deftly navigates the ship and lands it in a park not two blocks from Kaetlyn's home in Bantry, Ireland.

As Kaetlyn and Shamus step out, it feels oddly vacant and sanitized, like a hospital. The stench of death, which had permeated the land in the wake of Severnus, had disappeared, but so had the sense of life and animation which imbued it.

It occurs to Kaetlyn, as they walk, that a culture does have a life of its own, clearly manifested by the emptiness she now feels.

They are not the first to return to Bantry. Dozens of homesteaders have already come back to start up their lives again, and thousands more will soon follow.

When they step into the house, Claire O'Sullivan rushes forward and wraps her arms around Kaetlyn, nearly squeezing the life out of her as tears spill down her cheeks.

"I have missed you so much," she says with another squeeze.

Harry, despite his usual silent countenance, cannot help himself as he wraps an arm around his daughter. "Good to have you home, lass."

As Claire pulls away from her daughter, she looks to Shamus, "You're looking rather fetch'n and older too," she declares as she grabs their hands and drags them into the kitchenette.

Already prepared, is a plate with a small mountain of fresh-baked scones and a pot of hot tea.

Claire serves up the tea and then sits next to Harry, both still possessed by some sense of surrealism that after everything that has happened, the family is sitting together again, in their home – something no one could have imagined possible.

"Place looks good, mum," says Kaetlyn, trying to make conversation.

Claire shakes a shiver from her body. "Living in that camp, in Belgium, oooh," she discharges another shiver, "all I could think about was getting back here, to our home."

"So, how did it go?" asks Harry as he plucks a scone from the pile, dabs it with a good dose of butter and takes a bite.

Kaetlyn tips her head at him. "We released the pods with the bio-bots several days ago, if that's what you mean."

"Seems so … anticlimactic," says Claire,

"Yeah, well, it was. I authorized the drop, and L.I.N. executed the deployment of the pods in strategic locations around the world, all in …" she glances at Shamus.

"Less than six hours," he finishes her sentence."

"So … that's it, we just sit and wait for those little bastards to do their job," says Harry over a mouthful.

"Yup, that's it, dad."

"So, we can finally take a deep breath and relax?" says Claire.

"We're not out of the woods yet, mum" says Kaetlyn. "Assuming the bio-bots clean up the CO2 in the next six or so years, we still have to survive the effects of planetary warming in the meantime – and that is going to be nothing short of a massive effort."

"Yes, we know …" begins Claire, "we are already living on food rations, until the farms get back into operation and food distribution starts up."

"We'll survive it," declares Harry with a large smile as his hand spears for another scone, "as long as Claire can make scones and tea exists, we can survive anything."

3

In the weeks that follow, life takes on the semblance of normality for Kaetlyn.

She sleeps in the comfort of her own bed, enjoys home-cooked meals, takes walks, and engages in dialogues with D-TEKT, and most importantly, spends hours talking to her new-found friend, Karina Osipova, who is back in Russia tending to her own affairs.

The world seems to have forgotten about Star Girl, for now, at least – and Kaetlyn could not be happier about it.

L.I.N. had sent the drone back to the home world, and as instructed by Kaetlyn, she remains in orbit, a good distance from Earth, where no one, and no satellites, can get to her.

Kaetlyn is no novice to the game now, she is, in fact, a veteran of the war, and she knows that to leave the ship there too long will be an invitation to more trouble.

With a quick breakfast, she steps out into the bright spring sun, rolls her pink Vespa from the garage where it has sat for months, gives it a polish, and then sets off to her favorite spot.

Moments later she is leaning against the gravestone, her favorite one, with a warm sun in her face and an enjoyable book in her hand.

She tosses a casual glance at the proprietor of the gravestone. "Hope you don't mind," she utters with a grin and then taps her phone.

"D-TEKT, play something."

The music emits from her phone as she leans her head back against the gravestone and lets the sun warm her skin.

It has been months since she sat here, months during which the world had changed, months where she was forced to play a role that changed her too.

There was one thing that had not changed, a need for isolation.

Some people recharged their inner batteries through social interaction – Kaetlyn, admittedly a card-carrying introvert, boosted hers by being away from everything, and everyone, for a time.

Some hours later, as she steps into the house, the smell of freshly baked goods and fresh-brewed coffee tantalizes her stomach which lets out a subtle squeal of anticipatory delight.

However, it is often a red flag, heralding the fact that her mother is scheming something and intends on trapping her in the kitchen for a private dialogue.

Stepping around the corner, she is completely caught off guard.

"What's going on?" she asks as she approaches the group seated, shoulder to shoulder, around the kitchen table.

"Have a seat, dear, we just want to talk," says her mom.

Kaetlyn eases into the chair, flicking a questioning brow at Serena and Shamus, and then she locks on Colonel Desmond, sitting directly across from her.

“Sorry, lass,” begins Desmond, “but, we felt it was important to discuss this matter with everyone present.”

“What matter is that?”

He tips his head at her. “Your unannounced plans.”

A sigh passes her lips. “Hmm, I see, so word got out.”

Shamus, sitting closest to her, shrugs. “I didn’t leak it, promise.”

“Is it true?” asks her dad.

Kaetlyn is silent. She had planned to break the news to everyone in a different fashion, but now, she feels cornered.

“Yes,” she begins, “I’m going back.”

Claire O’Sullivan stifles a cry as her eyes tear up.

Harry’s jaw crimps tight as a vice.

Serena and Shamus remain unfazed by the statement; they already know about it and were sworn to secrecy by Kaetlyn.

Colonel Desmond responds without betraying his true feelings, maintaining a stoic and staunch military disposition as he speaks. “May I ask why?”

Kaetlyn draws a deep breath, exhales, and attempts a disarming shrug. “I don’t belong here.”

That statement evokes another wince and subtle cry from her mom, while Harry simply bolts down his upset even tighter.

"Look," she says, "I love you all, you know that." She turns to her mom who tries to stem the tears, unsuccessfully as they stream down her cheeks, like small rivulets. Kaetlyn reaches over and squeezes her arm. "You, and dad, are the best parents I could ever have hoped for. You protected me, you let me be who I was without judging me, you supported me, and I am so proud to call you, my parents."

Claire gushes, while Harry's face reddens with burgeoning grief.

For a moment, the room remains utterly silent, before her mom breaks it. "I know you've always felt out of place, but this is so … extreme,"

Kaetlyn shrugs. "Is it? Is it extreme that I was able to remember who I was in my past life, and because of that, we were able to do what we just did?"

No one answers.

"I'm not trying to find greener pastures or better people or anything," she continues. "You know I have felt like a fish out of water, and now, I know why. For my own sake, my own sanity, really, I need to go back, if anything to get closure."

"Do you plan on coming back?" asks Desmond.

"I do. Not sure exactly when, but that is the plan."

"And who have you made these plans with?" asks Colonel Desmond with a tip of his head.

Kaetlyn smiles. "You will know soon enough, Colonel."

Harry exhales, as if he has been holding his breath this whole time. "And what about you, lad?"

Shamus looks at Kaetlyn and then back to the others. "I am staying. I have other things in mind for my life, and …" he pauses, almost coyly, "I've met someone."

"Ah – the secret outs," says Serena as she pokes him in the ribs. "Been holding out on us, eh?"

"Well, hardly, I mean, yes. I was going to tell Kaetlyn about it first, but now seems as good a time as any."

Kaetlyn leans over and kisses him on the cheek. "Happy for ya, really."

Colonel Desmond leans back in his chair, caressing his cup of coffee as he speaks. "How soon do you plan to leave?"

Kaetlyn answers. "Assuming everything stays on track with the Net-Zero mandates, a month or so."

"How long have you been planning this?" asks Harry.

"I've been toying with it since the day this whole thing started, but it was only in the last couple months that I came to the decision."

"Did something prompt it?"

Kaetlyn grins. "Yeah, sort of."

"What?"

"I was invited to return."

"Invited?" asks Desmond with a turned brow.

"I don't want to say too much right now, but let's just say that L.I.N. has been reporting on matters here, and given the positive results so far, apparently they wanted to extend an invitation to me to come back." She tips her head at them. "I accepted."

"But… won't you stand out in that world too?"

Kaetlyn chuckles. "Not any more than a Black girl in a white Catholic community like Bantry," she smiles."

"So, you'll be the first…" begins Desmond.

"Humans? Yes, Colonel – we will be the first."

Her comment causes a sudden and taciturn gap in the dialogue, like a skipped step, or better yet, a skipped heartbeat.

"What does mean – "we'll be the first?"

Kaetlyn draws a breath as Serena reaches over and squeezes her hand. "It's okay, just say it."

"Karina Osipova, the Russian attaché, is also going."

That statement precipitates a surprised look on their faces, more so on Colonel Desmond's.

"The Russian is going with you, back to this … other world?" he says with incredulity painted on his face.

Kaetlyn nods. "Karina and I share a special bond. She comes from a similar background, we have similar aspirations and... well, we like each other."

Shamus twists his head her way. "Like as in…?'

"Aye," answers Kaetlyn with a smile. "Partners."

"As in, together, you know…?"

"Yes, Shamus, we love each other. We want to be together. It is the perfect partnership on all counts."

Shamus draws a deep breath and then smiles. "Well…shite, I didn't see that one coming, but then again, who am I to judge?"

Kaetlyn squeezes his hand. "Sorry, it just wasn't meant to be for us, this time."

Another moment of long silence ensues while her parents, and Desmond, reconcile the news.

"Will we hear from you?" asks Harry.

She places her phone on the table and taps it, "D-TEKT, call L.I.N."

A second later, and to their astonishment, a holographic image morphs with the face of L.I.N.

"Hi, Kaetlyn, or should I say, Captain?" she finishes with a brilliant smile.

"Hi L.I.N. Please explain how this will work."

"Certainly," says L.I.N. as she turns to face the others. "The commlink is a one-way link, meaning that we, or rather, Kaetlyn and Karina, will be able to contact those who have access to the comm device, but not the reverse, and …" she pauses with a raised brow, "the connection is secure so that no one can possibly, as you say, hack into the computer – which is ME."

"And this thing …" nods Harry with contempt for anything that assaults his old-school mentality, "works no matter how far away you are?"

"There could be some delayed responses, several seconds at most, but overall, yes," answers L.I.N.

"Just like Skype, only better," adds Shamus.

L.I.N. tips her head at him. "Unless Skype can provide three-dimensional visualization, such as this, then it is far better."

"So …" begins Claire with a tepid smile, "we can talk to you whenever we want?"

"Yes, mum, whenever you want to call, you can."

Claire sheds new tears, but this time they are happy ones.

O

The crew, from RTÉ, Ireland's largest television network, adjust the lighting and sound, as Dorothy Malone, the Irish Prime Minister, gets a final dose of facial powder.

She turns an eye to the woman powdering her face. "If you're trying to cover my wrinkles, you'll need a bucket of that stuff."

The makeup girl smiles, "No ma'am, this just helps take away the shine under the lighting."

A man approaches. "We've loaded your speech on the prompter, ma'am." He points. "Can you read that okay?"

Dot nods.

"Okay, everyone," he announces, "we're live in 60 seconds," and then turns to the PM. "Ready?"

"I am."

With a ten second silent countdown, Dot begins the live transmission to the world.

"Hello. Twenty-seven months ago, on a gray October morning, two events took place that changed our world. On that day, the Irish military exhumed an alien spacecraft embedded in a cliffside in coastal region of Ireland, and on that same day, an eighteen-year-old girl by the name of Kaetlyn O'Sullivan, who resided not more than forty kilometers from the site of that craft's discovery, revealed that she had been aboard that very craft when it crashed. Two storms of controversy were set in motion, one about the UFO, and one about the assertions made by a girl, that she had been aboard that very craft, died, and came back. While the story assaulted many of us, certainly shaking the stanchions of acceptability and mediocrity, in the months that followed, Kaetlyn O'Sullivan proved to us that her claims were neither delusion nor fake, but fact, and because of her courage to break through the barriers between her life as she knew it to be, and the one she once lived, our world now stands on the threshold of recovery from an imminent and irreversible apocalypse that would have otherwise eclipsed the human race and most other living creatures." The PM pauses, her eyes still fixed on the cameras but her mind drifting for just a second or two. "Like you, like so many people across the world, the events of the past two and a half years, have changed my perspective about what is important and what is not. We are seeing the dissolution of ethnic hatred, wars, and conflicts for the first time in known history; and most importantly, the amalgamation and solidarity of people from across the globe, working shoulder to shoulder, to fix our planet. We have also seen, for the first time ever, the unification of people as an unstoppable force – with the realization that the democratic process which we so sorely believed was represented in our governing systems, was failing us, and that rule by the people was not truly a fact – but fiction. Today, the people are demanding democratic representation and they know they have the power to make it happen, and if not, to remove those from office who refuse to provide it and protect it." She pauses yet again. "On this very morning, Kaetlyn O'Sullivan left in the same ship she arrived in twenty-one years ago. Before leaving, she asked me to read this message to you.

> *"Hello everyone.*
> *I hope you will excuse my absence, and our sudden departure this morning. No doubt, our disappearance will be fodder for the naysayers to make claims that we never existed, that intelligent life beyond our planet is not real, and that everything about me and this ship, was just an elaborate hoax. I am confident that you will see through their lies, and I am confident that the history books will reflect actuality, not some delusional narrative. Over the past many weeks, we have been engaged in dialogue with those who originally sent us on this mission. Sounds weird, I know, and believe me, at first, I was shocked, but when you accept the fact that there are other cultures out there, other beings*

just like you and I, well, it is like taking a phone call from across the stars – no big deal. Anyhow, two things resulted from those talks. First, they invited me to return. That was a difficult decision, because I consider this my home now; but the day I crossed over and opened the door to my past life, I bridged the gap to another world – showing me that we do not, cannot, have just one home – not as beings who live an infinity of lives. If you find this difficult to accept, it is only because you are trying to reconcile what you have been taught to believe. Listen to your soul, it never lies. The second thing that resulted from these talks, and what eradicated any doubts on my part about accepting their invitation was when they told me I could return to Earth one day and initiate another process called INFUSION - a specially prepared package of knowledge and technology which would be unilaterally introduced to Earth, to all nations and all people, to help advance its progress to the stars. What you do not know yet, and which I have barely been introduced to, is that there exists a federation of civilizations out there, within the context of the Milky Way alone; a constellation of cultures who work in alliance and symbiotic peaceful co-existence, and that is just one exceedingly small part of the Universe. The potential awaiting us is unbelievable. We have been led to believe that we are alone, just small unimportant creatures on a small planet on the edge of this galaxy, and nothing could be further from the truth. We are part of a grand choreography of sentient intelligent beings that spreads across the cosmos, all of it just waiting for humanity to step up to the threshold. I am not going back to my other home world to leave Earth for good. I am going there, in part to gain closure, and to negotiate on your behalf, so that I can return here some years into the future and introduce this package which will help boost our culture to the stars. In preparation for that day, there are conditions which they laid down, which they asked me to relate to you. These conditions must be met before we can return and introduce INFUSION.

- *Unilateral nuclear disarmament of ALL nations.*
- *The destruction of all nuclear military arsenals on Earth.*
- *All wars and conflicts ended.*
- *Net-Zero objectives accomplished with the complete resolution of global warming.*
- *The reformation of government platforms to the end of true democracy,*

that is, rule by the people, not rule by elitists or oligarchies or corrupt governments, in all nations on Earth.

These are things that most of us want. Only a small percentile of sociopaths and those with corrupt agendas will resist those conditions. We have time during the next six or seven years as the BioBots do their job of cleaning up the atmosphere, to put the above terms into play. Do not count on your governments to do this. They are temporary agencies at best, and you have already shown that you are the true and permanent power on Earth.

This world belongs to you. See you in the future.

- *Kaetlyn O'Sullivan*

Epilogue

"What am I looking at here?" asks the Chairman of the Joint Chiefs of Staff.

The Vice-Admiral of the Air Force points to the screen. "Live footage coming from iDrone."

Madox tips his head. "iDrone?"

Vice-Admiral Stevens, who stepped up and took charge of the Air Force when the President summarily demoted Admiral Willis, taps his pad and turns it for him to see.

"iDrone is an ADX developmental property, about the size of the tip of a pen and which uses alien technology we managed to repurpose from several alien crafts captured over the decades."

"But how did you get it aboard?"

"Before Admiral Willis was removed from office, he ordered them to figure out a way to get one or more of them onto the alien craft. Unfortunately, the iDrones, despite their size, were not able to penetrate further than the antechamber, which possesses a means of detecting and eliminating any foreign pathogens or the like. However, to its merit, one of the iDrones did manage to append itself to the outside hull."

"I will not even ask how that is possible. So," Madox nods at the computer, "How far away is that streaming now?"

"According to the last report I received before coming to this meeting, they are well past Pluto, approaching the edge of our solar system."

Madox leans forward, his eyes glued to the screen with astonishment. "So that little fucker is relaying that footage to us from that far away?"

"Yes, sir," answers Stevens.

Madox leans back in his chair, his head bobbing like a toy as he silently assesses the information.

"You're telling me, that with that thing attached to the alien craft, we might be able to track it to its final destination?"

Vice-Admiral Stevens nods. "This is a Beta rendition, sir, so I cannot guarantee anything. We don't even know if the footage will continue with this clarity once that ship gets light years away, but we're certainly hoping that the tracker will keep pinging, and eventually, that we will be able to determine its destination."

Admiral Madox stands and paces the room in silence before turning to the Vice-Admiral. "You do realize what this means, right, Stevens?"

"I think so."

"If we can track that ship to its home planet, it means we can get there some day and that means we don't have to fuck around with one ship anymore, we'll have access to their entire world – or worlds, according to Kaetlyn O'Sullivan's final message."

He smiles as he leans into the small conference table. "This is a game-changer, Stevens, and one that we cannot let out of the bag, you understand?"

The man nods.

"Do you think ADX is up to the task of building a ship that can travel there?"

Stevens raises a brow. "We have gleaned some technology from the other ships we have secreted away over the years. It is possible, I suppose."

"Good! You tell Rockwell Sims that ADX has a new priority mandate, to replicate a ship capable of getting us to this other world. And …" his finger points at the screen, "get our people onto mapping the exact itinerary taken by that alien craft so we can eventually follow it there."

The end (maybe)

Books by Réal Laplaine

Intrusion: A Keeno Crime Thriller (Book I)
Quantum Assault: A Keeno Crime Thriller (Book II)
The One: A Keeno Crime Thriller (Book III)
The 9th Divinity: A Keeno Crime Thriller (Book IV)
The Buffalo Kid
Finding Agnetha
See Me Not
Dead but not Gone.
Twilight Visitor
Earth Escape
Woman EX
The Other
L.I.N.
When Gods Roar: The Awakening
When Cowboys Fall
V.O.I.C.E. – The Silence is Over!

Visit the author website at

www.reallaplaine.com

www.ingramcontent.com/pod-product-compliance
Lightning Source LLC
LaVergne TN
LVHW050531160826
845677LV00011B/1989

* 9 7 9 8 2 3 0 8 2 5 1 8 0 *